HATES IT HERE

JUL 2 2 2019

Scarlett Epstein

HATES IT

HERE

BY **ANNA BRESLAW**

RAZORBILL

An Imprint of Penguin Random House

RAZORBILL

An Imprint of Penguin Random House
Penguin.com

ISBN: 978-1-59514-836-0

Printed in the United States of America

1 3 5 7 9 10 8 6 4 2

Book design by Corina Lupp

For my mom

prologue

THIS IS ONE OF THE HARDEST things I've ever had to write.

After five years, six seasons, ten Emmy nominations, and countless amazing experiences on and off the set with the family I've made here, the *Lycanthrope High* story has come to its conclusion. While I have no control over the decision, I could not be more proud of the extraordinary talent both in front of and behind the cameras who have collectively made this show what it is.

Write to the network if you want, but you know they're just a bunch of old white dudes in suits, right? All I'm gonna say is that they may or may not have almost fired me for making Connor Korean-American.

But look. You know that from the very beginning, I've been thinking about you guys—the superfans, the cosplayers, the people who wrote letters to me saying that Luke's death helped them with their own grief, or that Gillian and Reginald inspired them to end their abusive relationship, or that Marissa and Connor were the first complex main characters who looked like them that they'd seen on one of their favorite shows. That stuff means more to me than any critic's opinion.

And in my own bittersweet way, I'm glad to end here, while the characters are beloved and the plot hasn't jumped the shark. I don't want the show to overstay its welcome. It's kind of cool! Like the James Dean of shows, *very much* including the bisexual experimentation. (Wiki it.)

When you think about it, the ending is somewhat natural—graduation day was near, and then they were gonna go off to college. It's uncertain, yes, but life is uncertain. (Tangentially related: As most of you read on my blog, I have a new baby, and it turns out babies happen to be relatively high maintenance.)

It's been an incredible run, more than my seventeen-year-old nerdy self could have hoped for in his wildest dreams, and you guys are to thank for making it happen. I made this show for you. And don't worry. I'm counting the minutes—perhaps when the kid's older, anywhere between being a tiny poop monster and a thirty-four-year-old finally moving out of our basement—until I can make another one for you.

Not to get sappy, but all I did was tell people how to hold the camera. It's you guys who gave it a soul.

Be back soon. Promise.

—John St. Clair, creator of *Lycanthrope High*

chapter one

"IT ABSOLUTELY SUCKS," Avery says, beating out Jeffrey
Dahmer for the understatement of the century. (His, after his
arrest, was "I really messed up this time.")

Ave jams an impossible amount of textbooks into her
backpack. She's the only one in the whole hallway who cares
that the bell is ringing. It's kind of her personal brand.

She continues, "It one hundred and fifty percent sucks.
But—God, Scarlett, you look awful."

My eyes are puffy, and my throat's so sore from crying that
I can barely tell her "No shit." I stayed up all night with the rest
of the heartbroken *Lycanthrope* community, trying to strategize
a way to get it back on the air. The first stage is denial, right?
That's half of us, writing passionate letters to the network. The
other half—people I used to see on Tumblr every day—are
blackballing the show and moving on.

Not only was I one of the more popular fic writers on the board, but I'd livetweet the show every week at eight, amassing a pretty damn big following for a non-famous teenage girl who wasn't posting butt selfies. Every Monday from eight to nine P.M., I actually mattered. That was like my real life—all the stuff around it was just temporary, unfortunate background noise.

The worst part is, the sixth season finale didn't wrap anything up—it was some dumb monster-of-the-week about Greg's robot stepmom. We don't even know who ends up with whom. Even if John St. Clair tells us at some convention, which is what show runners generally do, it's not the same. He made the characters so real that it's simply unfair just to cut us off like this.

"I know you're bummed, but this means, maybe, just hear me out, that you can . . . invest in real people, not fictional people"—Avery sees what I am about to say and cuts me off— "and not a bunch of randos on a message board who are probably all sketchy old men."

"You really need to stop DVRing *To Catch a Predator*."

Ave should be more supportive, considering we first became friends when she sat behind me in AP English. I worked on *Lycanthrope* fanfics in my notebook and caught her reading over my shoulder. She reads for fun a lot; she's maybe the only person at school who does that as much as I do. But other than the architectural skill she displays by managing to fit every math textbook ever written in her book bag, Avery isn't at all artsy or creative. I think that's why we get along. Combined, we'd be Supergirl.

Ave is the only reason I can sit at the lunch table with the Girl Geniuses, a small clique of overachievers who run on Adderall and fear and have gears you can always see turning. No wonder they're maladjusted; it's uncomfortable seeing people try that hard, you know? Like, we don't want to see your gears. Put them away. It's their parents' fault for flogging them like the workhorse in *Black Beauty*. Take the shivering mess of Jessicarose Fallon, for instance. This summer her parents sent her on a "volunteer" trip to Argentina for a cool $5K so she could write a heart-wrenching college essay about how she ran out of Luna bars on day three. They also named her *Jessicarose*, so it's hard to fault her for having the eyes of a crazy person. In fact, a lot of the Girl Geniuses have a mash-up of two names, like Tanya-Lynn Gordonov. Perhaps their parents were on Adderall when they named them.

If you were wondering, I have a shining 2.9 GPA out of . . . I guess 4.0? Infinity? Whatever Jessicarose Fallon has.

"Okay, fine," Ave relents. "But have you considered maybe they're all just your Tyler Durden?"

I'm about to shoot back some sassy answer when Ave jerks her head in a quick spasm toward the end of the hall, where Gideon Maclaine is leaning against a locker and messing with his iPhone. He's alone, as usual.

"Look! A flesh-and-blood human," Ave says pointedly.

"Oh, *please*."

"You've been obsessed with him since the second grade!" She grins. "Maybe he can replace *Lycanthro*—"

"Don't say it. I can't even hear the title right now; it's too hard."

While the other girls at school threw themselves into boyfriends, I threw myself into shows. I started with the ones that are Taken Very Seriously, starring conflicted antiheroes who cheat on their wives and curse a lot, occasionally at the same time. But the problem was, I never really watched an episode and thought: *I want to mess around with these characters, bend their world, go inside their heads.* I usually just thought: *Sure. I get it. Men do coke and / or have sex with their twentysomething brunette mistresses but still love their kids or whatever.* I don't need to do a deep dive into that guy's head. I'm not someone that show thinks about.

Then I found *Lycanthrope High*, and everything totally changed. That sounds melodramatic, because I still have arms and legs, but everything *else* totally changed. It's about a boarding school called Pembrooke Academy where the student body is not-so-secretly 50 percent werewolves, and a scholarship student named Gillian finds out she's a *loup-orateur,* the only girl in her generation who can settle the war between werewolves and humans. There's a diverse cast of wisecracking misfits and love triangles and saving the world and all that good stuff.

Most of all, though, it's obvious—not just on the show, but in interviews and podcasts and at conventions—that John St. Clair thinks about me. Or, you know, girls like me. Amazingly, a straight white dude is designing his show specifically for bored, sexually frustrated high school girls (and some guys) who get straight Cs because their pointlessly large imaginations are uncontrollable tsunamis that wipe out any structure in their paths. For once, we don't have to adjust our expectations to wedge ourselves into an audience. We *are* the target audience. I love *Lycanthrope* and the characters down to my bones, in a way I can't even articulate, the way you love your family or your best friend.

Avery sat through one episode, one time, and thinks she gets the appeal but it's "not her style." Meanwhile, she made me and my mom, Dawn, sit through all thirteen episodes of *Cosmos*, and we were bored to tears, but on the bright side, we agreed on something for once. Dawn—a person who named her daughter after Vivien Leigh in *Gone with the Wind*, a person who watches reruns of *Sex and the City* so religiously that when I was little I used to confuse the theme for the eleven o'clock news—thinks *Lycanthrope High* is lame.

"I'm just trying to get you to look on the bright side!"

"Did you hit your head? We live in New Jersey. There is no bright side. If you want to use that expression here, you have to say, 'Look on the smog.'"

Melville, New Jersey, is the perfect place to have a pretty mediocre life for, like, seventy years and then die. In fact, that might be on the WELCOME TO MELVILLE sign you see when you get off the turnpike at Exit 6A, right above population: 5,500 EMPTY FUNYUNS BAGS, 1 BORED JEWISH GIRL.

As for Melville High School, where Ave and I go—it's

pretty much the opposite of magic. The English language isn't innovative enough to have a word for that, really, other than some four-letter ones I'm not going to deploy because I'm a ~*~LaDy~*~*. MHS is all guys with neck tattoos and girls who post Kim Kardashian quotes on Instagram, and the 60 percent of us who actually graduate end up working at Target or the gas station or something.

No thanks to Mr. Barnhill, our guidance counselor, whose soaring, inspirational college admissions advice is to "be realistic." (Some real *Chariots of Fire* stuff right there.) When Mr. Barnhill asked me how my extracurriculars were, I didn't say anything, because as far as school is concerned, I'm the president of the Misanthrope Society. Also the only member. He told me to consider community college, and I left with a pamphlet about identifying herpes.

You know the kind of person who rolls his or her eyes at a TV show or a book and goes, "That would *never* happen"? I'm the opposite: I walk around all day waiting for a reason to suspend my disbelief. There's a ghost in the girls' locker room? Great; let's find out if she's a murdered former prom queen out for revenge. The entire town of Melville, New Jersey, is directly over the Eighth Circle of Hell? Awesome. I shotty the crossbow.

When school lets out, I race back home to check my permanently open *Lycanthrope* tabs. As I'd feared, the boards have been swarmed with the worst kind of invasive awfulness: TV critics looking to interview "heartbroken cult fans" for articles. (No thanks—I've never seen fandom portrayed in any mainstream place as anything other than a weird cult, and fangirls as brainless idiots.) There are also countless culture bloggers shamelessly spamming the board with links to their immediately-churned-out "Best *Lycanthrope High* Episodes" roundups. Here and there, I do see some fix-its—fanfiction revisions of the end of the series—but none by my friends.

My best friends in the *Lycanthrope* fandom community are called the BNFs (Big Name Fans), and they're fic writers too: xLoupxGaroux, DavidaTheDeadly, and WillianShipper2000. Fandom is weird like that, especially on Tumblr. You don't have to know anyone's first name, but you'll be as sad for them when their mom dies as you'd be sad for someone IRL.

I gravitated to them through their super-high-quality fics. They were the top-read *Lycanthrope* fic writers on the board; their most popular fics had around 10,000 views. xLoupxGaroux appeals to the smart, snarky gay demo who dies for William/Connor slash with only occasional glimmers of sentimentality. DavidaTheDeadly writes uplifting inner monologues from each character's perspective, which gives people a break from the frequent super-darkness of the show. And Willian, a high school freshman in Kansas, excels at maybe the toughest and most oversaturated fanfic domain: your typical OTP (one true pairing) hetero romance. She splits her time between *Lycanthrope* and One Direction fandom, and she sometimes comes off totally basic, but her swoonworthy lines get Tumblr-ed to death. Some

Lycanthrope fans can be judgy about mainstream fandoms like 1-D, but I'm not: Anything that could get a sixteen-year-old girl from some shitty town a six-figure book deal is something I'd scream proudly about from the rooftops.

> **xLoupxGaroux: Where have you BEEN.**
>
> **Scarface: I'm sorry!!**

I start crying. I'm not quite sure why. I think I'm afraid this is the last time we'll all talk or something. Nevertheless, I manage to type:

> **Scarface: I'm crying, hahaha!**
>
> **xLoupxGaroux: you are not literally crying.**
>
> **DavidaTheDeadly: we don't all have hearts of stone like you, Loup**
>
> **Scarface: Yes**
>
> **WillianShipper2000: awwwww!**
>
> **DavidaTheDeadly: last week I cried every day. moaning myrtle of the ladies' bathroom at work basically.**

Davida and Loup are both older than me and have office jobs, which means they can—and do—Gchat all day but have to be careful with the open browsers.

DavidaTheDeadly: the thing is though . . . we didn't know it was ending, and we don't have source material for fics about the final episodes. oh brb boss is coming

xLoupxGaroux: What is it today? "Ride of the Valkyries"?

DavidaTheDeadly: "Single Ladies."

Whenever the editor in chief at Davida's magazine job approaches someone's cube, Davida hums loudly to warn them to X out of anything inappropriate.

DavidaTheDeadly: haha btw scarface, pls thank your mom for e-mailing her confession and let her know it'll be in the april issue

The delightful nugget to which she is referring: "I wrote a text to my ex-boyfriend: 'I'll pick up some condoms with the bread bowls.' But I actually sent it to my daughter! Oops! —Dawn E., 35."

Scarface: I can't believe we don't even know if Gillian ends up with William or Connor.

WillianShipper2000: Uhh Willian is obvs the OTP!

Willian's ride-or-die for that pairing. Her Tumblr background is a shot of the two of them with "Now you have all of me" written on it in cursive, from that episode where William and Gillian had a big fight because he wouldn't take her to prom. He wanted her to have a nice, normal teenage experience. She started crying and said he was letting the wolf part—the part that didn't like responsibility—take over. The next day he showed up at her front door with a gift, a German shepherd puppy. "You were right," he said. "But now you have all of me."

(Of course, Gillian realizes later on, when William leaves town after prom, that it was the guy part of him that decided to do it, not the wolf part. And the dog, Nina, dies bravely saving Marissa from a possessed frat house in the fourth season finale. I cried for a week straight.)

Scarface: Have you guys read any of the fix-its?

xLoupxGaroux: Some—none are particularly satisfying.

We agree that none of us want to give up writing *Lycanthrope* fic and that even though the finale sucked, moving forward we'll stick with the canon storyline. We all promise to think on it, and nobody will jump ship until we've got some ideas.

chapter two

"MY CHILDREN," I BEGIN SOLEMNLY at the head of the Parkers' dinner table.

The first time I had dinner at Avery's house, in sixth grade, her parents asked me to say grace in earnest. But after I fumbled secularly through it, the BS "grace" became a recurring joke.

I clear my throat. "I dreamed I was walking on the beach side by side with the Lord. When I looked back, there were two sets of footprints, but other times there was just one."

Ashley, Avery's sister and the bane of my existence, rolls her eyes. I ignore her.

"I asked the Lord why this would be. He replied, 'During your times of trial and suffering, when you see only one set of footprints, it was then that I drop-kicked you.'"

The tops of Avery's parents bowed heads shake with silent laughter.

"Carried you. Carried you, is what I meant. Amen."

"Amen," Avery and her parents say. Ave's mom looks at Ashley expectantly, and she reluctantly mutters it too.

Ashley's a popular senior at MHS. She and her friends have spent the last nine years making fun of me for wearing thrift-store clothes (they weren't cool yet), bringing weird wholesale Sam's Club chocolate milk to lunch unlike everybody else's normal Nesquiks, and the million other tiny indicators kids can sniff out poorness with. The most glaring example of this was in second grade, when all the popular girls had Double Stuf and I had some cheaper fake-Oreo brand; I'd scrape all the cream off one cookie and put it in another, then throw out the dry, empty cookie and eat the homemade Double Stuf one. One day, Natalia and Ashley sat across from me and stared as Ashley whispered unnecessary narration into Natalia's ear like I was a nature documentary. *Look, then she scrapes the cream off, then she puts it in the other cookie, then she throws the first cookie out, then . . .*

Since I became friends with Avery and close with her parents, the teasing has been like a long game of chicken: Was I going to rat on her, or was she going to stop siccing her Ugg-booted henchwomen on me? So far, neither has happened. Ave just stays out of it.

Even after nine years of torture, though, Ashley's prettiness still stuns me like a manta ray. She looks like a Disney princess, pale with fiery red hair and a perfect ski jump nose, and stops just short of being *too* beautiful, as if God designed her to provide a believable photo for catfishing people. Ave is pretty too, but she's like a wilted version of Ashley with braces and slightly duller hair. If they had been fetal twins, Ashley definitely would've consumed Avery for nutrients, and all that'd be left of Ave would be a tumor with a few teeth in it.

Ave's mom gets up with some plates. "Salmon, anybody?" She explains to me, "We're doing the Grain Brain diet, but I think I have some spelt crackers in the cupboard if you want."

"Thanks, I'm okay."

"Have you read about that? Wheat, carbs, and sugar destroy brain cells. Even quinoa," she says, glancing at Avery's dad quickly to make sure she recited it correctly. Professor Parker teaches a graduate class on nutrition at Princeton. The only noise at the table is the oppressive clinking of silverware. They're the total opposite of me and Dawn—we're either screaming at each other or laughing hysterically, big emotions that ricochet off the walls of our apartment.

"Little late for me, I think," I reply.

"Scarlett, you know you're very bright," Professor Parker says brusquely, which is how he says most things, even compliments.

Ashley lets out a sharp breath of air from her nose, a mean, soundless laugh. Her mom gives her a warning glare.

"Listen, I understand that you don't care about doing well in school right now, but there are a handful of colleges known especially for their exemplary creative-writing programs. Just get that GPA up, and your writing will speak for itself. You're very talented," he continues.

I feel my face burning, especially considering I haven't really written since the show went off the air. The Parkers make everything sound so purposeful, as if I set out To Write, or to Be a Writer. Writing is just the only thing that makes me feel like a real person, not the tap-dancing reflection of myself that I am around other people. Until *Lycanthrope High* ended, I'd find ways to write all day at school, like on the backs of handouts in class or hidden in the stacks of the school library between AMERICAN HISTORY (A–P) and AMERICAN HISTORY (P–Z). It didn't seem odd or unique to me that by the time sophomore year was over, I'd written a novel-length fic.

Besides the BNFs, Avery was the only person I told, and she talked me into letting her read it. Of course she told Professor Parker, and then *he* read it, and I was super-embarrassed and mad at Ave because it had all kinds of teenage hedonism in it and what have you. And when he finished, he called Dawn and told her that I had an immense talent and there were creative arts high schools specifically for students like me and he'd send over some pamphlets. Dawn was so pissed—she said he was trying to give me "champagne taste on a beer budget."

The truth is, part of why I started writing is that it's one of the few activities that doesn't require any expensive helmets or gear or pay-by-the-hour instructors. And Dawn's right, we can't afford any of those schools Professor Parker mentioned, but I can't say stuff like that to the Parkers, because underneath this conversation, they know it, and they know *I* know it, and articulating it would just make things weird. I already think sometimes that I perform for them a little too much, constantly trying to be funny and charming, like I'm singing for my supper or something.

Instead, I try to stop blushing and shrug like *zero shits given*.

"Frankly, I think MHS is a bad fit for both of you," says Mrs. Parker, and she gives Avery a pointed look. Freshman year, Avery's parents made her go to a fancy, expensive boarding school in Massachusetts. She hated it there, but they refused to let her come home until she resorted to drastic measures: A few days before summer break, she tagged along with some girls in her hall to get their belly buttons pierced. One not-so-accidental crop top later, Avery was matriculated at MHS for sophomore year.

As Ave's parents start grilling her about SAT prep, Ashley's phone chimes with a text, and she snatches it off the table.

Kevin Rice, Avery mouths at me. That would be Ashley's latest conquest, who graduated MHS last year but eschewed college in favor of landing a record deal with his screamo band. I forget the name. It's like Burgermaggot, or Juicewater, or some other two-word gibberish that sounds like you're having a stroke when you say it.

Ashley beams as she reads the text message. You can practically hear the cartoon bluebirds chirping around her head. He wears eyeliner, for God's sake.

"Light of my life. Fire of my loins," I say quietly, and watch Avery snort gratifyingly into her salmon. Professor Parker stifles a laugh, but Ashley sees his eyes are squinty and smiling.

"Dad, you're being annoying."

He straightens himself out.

"It's not even him anyway," says Ashley, then a little quieter: "You assholes."

"Language, Ashley Nicole," Mrs. Parker says on autopilot.

"Buttholes," she says, then gets up and storms to her room.

If Kevin's out, that means she has someone else in rotation. Ashley, as everyone at MHS knows, has a pattern. She goes out with a different guy every other week, and every time it ends, it's The Most Dramatic Thing That's Ever Happened. She winds up in the girls' bathroom crying, smoking a wrinkled Virginia Slim she stole from her mom's purse, then covering it up by spraying enough Gap Dream to choke livestock. Ave once went in right after her, and she almost had an asthma attack.

Ashley, Avery says, then swears to Never Love Again (she's one of those every-first-letter-capitalized kinds of feelings-havers) and Focus on School and Cheerleading and How Hashtag-Blessed She Is until some other boy who has a car asks her if she wants to "chill." Then they make out in the back row of *The Even Faster & Even Furiouser* and she comes home with her shirt on inside out, In Love Again.

After Avery and I help clear the table, we go to her room so she can "tutor me in math," otherwise known as "read *Rookie* and play F-Marry-Kill while drinking seven hundred Diet Cokes from the mini-fridge."

As we pass Ashley's closed door, we hear a pealing laugh. Even her laugh is perfect.

"Who's the new dude?" I ask.

"I have no idea, Scarlett," Ave informs me in the sweetly patient tone she always uses when I'm looking for Ashley intel, like how you might talk to a three-year-old. "I'm not on whatever review board she presents her biweekly meat to."

"You know who your sister reminds me of?"

Ave nods, waiting.

"Patience. Hot, popular valedictorian. Secretly a three-thousand-year-old demon bent on world destruction."

That's one of the things I liked most about the *Lycanthrope* universe: Everyone who is beloved here, you can bet they're evil there. That works in reverse too. John took trope-y archetypes and turned them upside down; nobody's ever what you'd expect them to be.

Ave humors me. "What happens to her?"

"She gets beheaded by a giant pair of ancient scissors."

"Uh, really?"

"Yeah, they're the only thing that can—just forget it, okay?"

As close as Ave and I are in some ways, there's a layer of our friendship way underneath where we split apart. She lives inside rules, angles she can draw with a protractor or determine with her graphing calculator. Sometimes I miss having a best friend who totally gets me.

chapter three

GIDEON'S BEEN IN THE SAME CLASS as me since pre-K, the chubby boy in the XL Old Navy polo sitting way in the back, doodling manga on the back of his English tests, but like me, he's invisible.

My crush on him began in second grade, which is not quite as creepy as it sounds. It was circumstantial, initially—my dad spent afternoons working on his book, and Dawn's shift at TGI Fridays started at two P.M. Mrs. Maclaine offered to pick me up with Gideon and watch me after school. Neither of us were outgoing, and at the center of both of our friendlessness was an overlap, like a Venn diagram: He was weird because he was shy, and I was weird because I was poor.

Initially, the arrangement was cool only because Gideon's family is rich. They live in a big house, similar to the ones Dawn cleans, and his dad's a plastic surgeon in the city. We could hang out in his giant rec room, or float in the swimming pool, or plunk in front of the flat-screen TV while devouring his mom's homemade snacks. (That alone was a treat. The Maclaines eat farm-to-table; the Epsteins eat freezer-to-table.)

As I got older, I became more embarrassed about how Dawn was always twenty minutes late to pick me up, smelling like mozzarella sticks, with her tchotchke-pinned apron slung over the passenger seat. Then I'd feel guilty for dreading it. That was when I first started writing, trying to unravel feelings I couldn't really talk about.

By eighth grade, Gideon was still a foot shorter than every other boy in class; he trudged and wove through the hallway like a Frogger nobody paid attention to. I still got straight Cs and had no idea how to talk to other people. School was just a forced, lame interlude between our real worlds, our various obsessions, and our friendship. We both watched *Lycanthrope* religiously. We'd even Gchat after each episode, incredulous about what we'd just seen—but I never told him about my fanfic friends. I was afraid that would cross some invisible weirdness line.

The turning point was the swelteringly hot summer between eighth and ninth grade, the year our parents left books on our beds with titles like *Your Body Is Changing and It's Normal (Not Witchcraft)*. It was the best summer of my life, probably—the last one before we drifted apart freshman year, for a number of reasons, many of which were established on this one particular day.

We were sitting on the giant leather couch in his cushy

central-air-conditioned basement, eating Oreos and watching a stack of old *Saturday Night Live* "best ofs" from the 1970s that Gideon slowly built up through Christmas and birthday presents every year. Gideon was the only person I could share that kind of comfortable silence with, without feeling compelled to make dumb jokes to fill it.

Neither of us understood a bunch of the references on old-school *SNL* episodes, but it felt dangerous somehow, different from anything we'd seen at the movies. The way Gideon watched John Belushi hurl himself at a wall reminded me of how I'd always read my favorite lines from books out loud, savoring the taste of them. That day, after a particularly long vintage Steve Martin binge, I finally asked him.

"Is this what you want to do?"

He turned bright red. "What do you mean? I don't know," he stammered, then asked again, as if he was short-circuiting, "What do you mean?"

"Like, comedy?"

"I . . . sometimes think I want to. But it's so silly. It's not a viable career path."

It really bothered me when he did that, echoed things his dad said to him like they were gospel. As far as Mr. Maclaine was concerned, anything that wasn't med school wasn't a viable career path.

"It's just dumb," he said softly.

"It's not dumb at all!"

"It's something I think about. Not, like, a lot." In Gideon-speak, that meant *obsessively*. It went way further than just *SNL*: Gideon watched every stand-up special on the air, pirated hard-to-find ones off the Pirate Bay, obsessively watched his favorite comics, and—as I realized once when I glanced at him in the middle of a Chris Rock special—took notes on the rhythms of the jokes, how the lineup came together, which segues felt natural and which felt forced.

"Why don't you try it?" I prodded. "Stand-up?"

"Like at the school talent show, you mean? There's a reason why I barely say anything in class. Do you really think anyone else from school is sitting here watching this stuff?"

"Maybe some of the teachers. The old ones."

He smiled and glanced at the stack of DVDs. "You actually kinda remind me of her," he said. "Gilda."

"Really?" I stared down at the carpet, crestfallen that he thought my doppelgänger was Roseanne Roseannadanna.

"Yeah. I don't know. You look sort of like her, I guess—in old pictures, when she's not in costume. But mostly . . . you kind of think like her. I don't know how to say it. Your mind, or your thoughts or something, they're just different from most people's."

"Thanks," I mumbled, goose bumps shooting up my arms and legs. It was, and remains, the best compliment I'd ever gotten.

"I wish I was more like that," he said quietly.

"So just try it! What's the harm? It'll suck for five minutes. School sucks for, like, eight hours a day. It's nothing."

"I dunno. I just feel like . . . it's all been done. There's nothing I can do that won't be a total knockoff of someone who's better." He sighed.

I almost blurted out that I felt that way about making up stories, but I bit my tongue at the last minute—too embarrassing. Which is strange, now that I think about it, because before that summer, I'd tell him everything, down to the last unappetizing, unflattering detail.

I adamantly unstuck my thighs from the leather sofa.

"Well, I'm not letting you start high school without trying it."

He looked for a second like he was considering it, drumming his long, thin fingers thoughtfully on his denimed thigh. Then he rolled his eyes, giving me his signature wide-eyed *You're being batshit* look.

"Where am I gonna go, Scarlett? The Yuk Machine?"

The Yuk Machine was (and still is, because nothing changes here—it's like a lamer Brigadoon) right off the highway in a strip mall, wedged between a liquor store and a ShopWay.

"This is a terrible, terrible, *terrible* idea." Gideon paced in the parking lot, drenching his sneakers in dirty puddles.

I gazed up at the neon sign. The *Y* was burned out.

"Actually, the Yuk Machine is a terrible idea," I said. "The Uk Machine is the best idea I've ever had."

Inside the dim club, I fiddled nervously with the neon under-21 bracelet, my Converse squishing against the inexplicably damp floor. The Yuk Machine would not have seemed out of place on the set of *Children of Men*. But when I glanced at Gideon, he was beaming like a cancer kid on a pamphlet for the Hole in the Wall Gang Camp. He was really gonna do this. In a flash, I was way more nervous than he was.

"Nobody's, like, parents are here, right?" he whispered.

I got on my toes and twisted to and fro to check for nosy Melville housewives. Instead of him helping me look, I felt him subtly glance me up and down, quick and fluttery like a moth, as if I was some random girl walking by him on the street and we hadn't been best friends for almost seven years. It gave me a little shiver. In a good way, I realized.

We quietly slunk to a small, wobbly table in the back and waited for the guy onstage to finish his set.

". . . alimony, right? I mean . . . what, even?" the guy was saying. Then he sighed and drank half his beer. Gideon and I winced at each other. At least he wouldn't be a tough act to follow.

Finally he finished, and the depressed-looking emcee came back on.

"Anybody else want to try their hand at open mic night?"

Gideon stood up.

"Oh, good," the emcee intoned in his flat, dead voice. "A child."

Finally, some laughs. Gideon faltered, and for a second I really wanted to kick that guy in the balls. But Gideon ambled up to the stage and jumped on anyway, taking the mic from the emcee.

"Hi, guys," Gideon said placidly.

I noticed my nervous leg-jiggling was shaking my little table. I stopped, then unthinkingly started biting my inner cheek instead.

He took a deep breath. "So, I'm forty-two, and . . ."

"Bullshit!" shouted a drunk man in the back.

Gideon smirked, winked, and became someone other than himself. "Thanks, man. Appreciate that. Nice to hear I can still pass for thirty." He paused for the giggling from various parts of the room.

He unhooked the mic from its stand and walked haltingly across the black stage, seeming to be in deep thought. My heart was pounding. I felt like it was me up there, squinting beyond the lights.

"Uh, so my parents are still together. . . . Um, thanks?" he said to the smattering of applause. "I'm just gonna point out that you have no idea what kind of marriage you just applauded, by the way."

Self-effacing laughs. Gideon was totally different up there. Relaxed, calm, self-assured. He even looked a little taller.

"But no, it's a good marriage. Of course they do fight sometimes," he continued. "Probably no more than normal. They grew up pretty different. That's part of it, probably. He grew up Irish-Italian, pretty strict family. He's been in therapy for a long time and gotten past a lot of that stuff. My mom grew up as a piece of wood and some fabric, and now she's an ottoman."

He had said it so casually that you'd almost miss it if it wasn't so odd. There was dead silence, but he continued deadpan, like he hadn't said it. Confused laughter from a few parts of the room. I remember literally holding my breath.

"It's a really romantic story. So my dad fixes old furniture for a living. They locked eyes across the secondhand store one day, and that was it. He had her reupholstered, her legs polished—the kind of ottoman he could see himself marrying. I mean, of course he says that she was already that ottoman on the *inside*. He just wanted her to have the upholstery to match because she deserved it."

Then suddenly, I got it. He *was* being personal; he just wasn't being literal.

"Isn't that a romantic story? It's just like *The Notebook*, if you swapped out Rachel McAdams for an extraneous piece of living room decor that's an afterthought to most people."

Big burst of laughter, sweeping Gideon along with it—but he allowed himself only a chuckle. ("I hate when comedians have that fake little laugh right before a bit, like they're being swept away by how awesomely funny this memory was. It's so obvious," he once mumbled with a mouthful of popcorn as we tore through the miserable collected works of Dane Cook "for research.")

Gideon stopped, abruptly breaking the rhythm, and stared at a point behind me. His face said: *Oh, shit.* I twisted around fast.

And there was Mrs. Maclaine, sticking out like a sore thumb

in an Hermès scarf (I once called it "a HER-mees," like *herpes*, and she corrected me: "an er-MEZ"), standing next to the bar with her arms crossed and looking very, very angry.

Five minutes later, Gideon and I sat on the damp curb, still so adrenaline-jazzed that we barely even cared we were in trouble. Meanwhile, Mrs. Maclaine stood by her BMW and called what seemed like every parent in Melville to let them know that we weren't going halfsies on a crack pipe. Her hand shook a tiny bit. The only reason she hadn't peeled off with Gideon was to wait for Dawn to come pick me up.

"I just knew when I came on they were all looking at me like 'Oh, no, here we go, it's a kid who's gonna joke about why high school sucks,' and I just . . . I wanted to prove them wrong."

"You were so, so funny. I was really nervous on your behalf, so I only laughed a few times, but . . ."

"I wanted to surprise the hell out of everybody in the room, you know?"

I shook my head. "You didn't."

He looked hurt. "Really?"

"*Almost* everybody. But I wasn't surprised at all."

We both looked out at the gleaming puddles spotting the parking lot in front of us, then beyond, to the freeway. The mutual high was fading, and we were back in our own lives again.

"I hate it here," he mumbled.

I just stared at the pavement. There was so much I could say. But I just whispered, "Me too."

He turned toward me, a familiar face but in a really

unfamiliar way, his green eyes locked on me. He moved his head closer to mine, and it felt so right that I'd already closed my eyes.

"Gideon Andrew Maclaine, you get in this car *right now*."

Headlights beamed onto us as a second car swished through the puddles to a crawl. A really shitty car. Dawn's car.

As I headed toward it, Mrs. Maclaine tapped on Dawn's window, her car keys entwined in her perfectly manicured hands—claws, I thought meanly—and Dawn cranked the squeaky handle until the window rolled down.

"Ms. Epstein, I know you've got *a lot going on*," Mrs. Maclaine said to my mother, her words dripping with disapproval, "but your daughter is out of control, and I certainly can't parent *for you*. Please find somewhere else to send Scarlett after school. I'm done."

With that, she slid into the driver's seat of her BMW, where Gideon was already waiting. Behind the tinted black glass, I saw he was looking straight ahead, blank. They glided out of the parking lot and onto the highway.

I got in the car. Dawn glared at me, shaking her head.

"Don't pull this shit with me, Scarlett. I already have enough to deal with."

I didn't say anything. I wanted to stay in that moment where Gideon was up there doing something so much better than just fitting in. Or in that moment on the curb when he came close enough that I could see the little flecks of brown in his green eyes.

Dawn yanked on the stick shift until it got into the right gear, and we headed home.

I stared out at the moon drifting alongside us, darting behind telephone poles and back out, but all I saw was the way Mrs. Maclaine had looked at me, like I was a speck of dirt on her countertop. I thought about how families like the Maclaines have big empty spaces between one another, while families like me and Dawn are smooshed on top of each other, hearing everything the other one's doing, barely being able to breathe our own air. The Maclaines have the latest, sleekest cars and phones. Nothing's ever an old model, something straining or squeaking or clicking, nothing about them ever invokes the ultimate embarrassing concept of *trying*. They have a beautiful silk curtain over the various awkward, rusty embarrassments of being human, and we don't.

That was the night the Maclaines decided, definitively, that I was a bad influence, and also when I realized that Gideon never seemed to contradict them. For the first time, I felt a wedge between us. He wouldn't stick up for me, I worried, for reasons that felt bigger than our friendship, reasons that had to do with how his mom looked at my mom in the parking lot. And honestly, just thinking that made me mad at him—that worst-case scenario I'd assembled in my mind.

After that, our friendship reversed—the conversations trickled backward into generic pleasantries, then nothing. We went from best friends to just faces that passed each other in the hallway. In the years since we'd drifted apart, Gideon got taller and fitter, going from soft and chubby to large and solid in a man-ish way that makes my hormones do a Mexican hat dance.

I stayed the same. Size six and five-foot-seven in heels (that I do not own). I pretty much wear a couple of different varieties of Old Navy clearance items and my dad's baggy dress shirts with leggings. I still wear the bras and underwear I've worn since, like, seventh grade. And every time I try on bras or jeans in a department store and some saleswoman says they fit me "right," they feel so tight I can't breathe, so I size up, because the patriarchy.

I have dark hair and gray-brown eyes. My dad's Jewish, and Dawn is half Mexican, so I either have skin you'd call olive or skin you'd call "jaundiced yellowy but with a great dark tan in the summer." My face is, I don't know, face shaped? I have to wear glasses, which sucks, but I did pick some bomb pink plastic grandma glasses from the Walmart Vision Center.

Gideon may not broadcast it like I do, but he's still weird. I know he is. Not like one of those kids who skulks around the band hallway proclaiming their strangeness with T-shirts, but a quiet, unshowy weird, like a slightly crooked picture frame. There's only one other guy I've liked, and it was Coach Taylor from *Friday Night Lights*, so that wasn't gonna end with a spring wedding.

The problem is, even though so much time has gone by since we've been friends, whenever I'm around him, I still feel entitled, demanding, and greedy, kind of like Veruca Salt from *Charlie and the Chocolate Factory*. I might miss social cues occasionally, but even I know that *We're supposed to be together. There's no reason I shouldn't come right out and say it, we've already wasted a lot of time, and would you like to do everything-except-sex with me?* is not an ideal opener.

But mostly it's scary because thinking about how I felt when I hung out with him is really close to how I feel when I'm writing. Like there are a million pegs but only one that fits in this weird hole, and I'm the hole, and writing is the peg. And Gideon is like another, um . . . peg. Hi, metaphor.

After skimming the boards—more bad fix-its, more nosy bloggers—I decide to Gchat Loup about my problem.

> **xLoupxGaroux: What do you mean? You can't write anymore?**
>
> **Scarface: i just sit there and stare at the screen like the missing link. I need STRUCTURE. I need you guys!**
>
> **xLoupxGaroux: Whoa. You weren't kidding about that PMS, were you, sweetie? Look. It was comfortable writing *Lycanthrope* fics because it was a pre-built world, with pre-built characters. But maybe you're having trouble building your own because . . . well**
>
> **Scarface: uh yes?**
>
> **xLoupxGaroux: You don't seem to get out much. I mean,**

you have to LIVE in order to write well about life, you know? Tolstoy didn't spend the first 30 years of his life on the sofa watching Hulu Plus and then out of nowhere write *Anna Karenina*.

Scarface: i get your point.

xLoupxGaroux: Do something crazy. Go ask out a boy.

Scarface: oh shit. no way.

xLoupxGaroux: Yes way. I will if you will!

Scarface: it's SO much worse in high school! people talk about who's dating with such GRAVITY, like they're talking about wikileaks.

xLoupxGaroux: If you don't I'll jump ship, swear to God. Lots of good slash OTPs for that CW show *Imaginary Detectives* . . .

Scarface: JESUS. Okay. Fine, I'll do it.

xLoupxGaroux: Good. Honor system.

chapter four

I MARCH OVER TO GIDEON, my heart pounding, feeling all the blood rush up to my head as I get closer. What the hell. After all, the first time Ted Hughes met Sylvia Plath, she bit him on the cheek, and he married her anyway. And they lived happily ever after.

"Hey," I say. He looks up from his phone.

"Oh, hey," he says in that neutral, accommodating voice you get when some stranger's about to ask you for directions. When I don't say anything, he asks, "Um, do you, like, need something?"

"It sucks about the show, right?" I blurt out.

"What show?"

"Lycanthrope High." For the first time, the name of the show sounds dumb and cringey coming out of my mouth, like how I'd imagine it would feel if I said the title of something I wrote myself.

"Oh." He sort of shrugs. "Sure, I mean, I watched it when it was on. I wasn't, like, a superfan or anything." It is hard to tell whether he's being honest or following the high school commandment of *Thou shalt not show thy uncoolness by openly caring about something*, which I have never been good at.

"Okay, look. Imagine your life without access to comedy. That's what it feels like. It's so boring that even small, momentary escapes are in full Technicolor, like flirting with an older guy with a big calf tattoo at the gas station. It's worse than boring, actually, because it's not like you're sitting in a waiting room, flipping through *Redbook*. I mean, that's boring, but at least you'll eventually get called in to your appointment. Whereas life is boring, but unless you're suicidal or a Scientologist, the waiting and the appointment are the same thing—you know? Isn't that how you'd feel?"

—What I want to say.

"Oh. Dope."

—What I actually say.

Another weird long silence, the opposite of the knowing ones we used to have when we were kids, during which I pray for Aaron Sorkin to swoop in and write my life for the next two minutes (sans the cis-hetero-white-male-on-a-soapbox part).

"I—do you want to do something sometime?"

He looks surprised. "Uh . . ."

"I know it's been a really long time since we hung out, but I think we still, you know, we like the same stuff, and we're both . . ."

The look in his eyes stops me, like I was about to say "serial killers" or "Coldplay fans." Shit. Come on, try again. I can be articulate. Go.

"You know, like how you and I both . . ." His blank look makes me falter again. I wave to vaguely indicate the hallway, the school, the town, the world. "Don't you still feel like you don't really . . ."

"What? Fit in?"

"I mean . . . yes? No. Sort of."

A mix of confusion and annoyance clouds his face. Why did I think this was a good idea?

"I don't feel like that."

"Okay, um, I'm sorry."

"That was a long time ago. You know? I mean, we haven't hung out in, like . . ." He is so weirded out, he can't even finish the sentence.

"Yeah, no, totally," I mumble, backing away.

He shrugs. "So, I'm good now. Plenty o' friends. Thanks for your concern, though."

My face feels like it's on fire. I back off and hurry away. In the back of my head, though, I'm thinking, *Nobody who has plenty of friends would say "plenty o' friends."*

Just when I'm about to speed-walk around the corner, I glance back at Gideon, and with my head turned, I smack directly into Ashley.

"Oh, sorry," I mumble.

"No, I am soooo sorry," she says, knitting her on-trend thick eyebrows with overwrought concern, and continues down the hall. She has less of a walk than an easily imitable busty glide, leading with the kind of boobs that prompt dim boys like Mike Neckekis to deem her "really smart" or "really funny."

And then she takes a running leap into Gideon's arms.

chapter five

RUTH IS DYING LAUGHING, which is even making Avery crack up a little, and I don't appreciate it.

"It's not funny." I shove the bulb into the crude trowel hole I made a few moments ago. "First the show, now this. All of a sudden my whole life is just a shit salad."

"Pointed side *up*, milady!" Ruth shouts from her end of the garden, wiping sweat off her brow and accidentally replacing it with dirt. She grabs her lighter—a gold one, with an engraving I've never dared get close enough to read—and sparks up a J.

Ruth is seventy-three. Did I mention that?

I roll my eyes and turn the bulb right-side up. Avery's curled up in the hanging chair on the porch with a calculus workbook, having put in her thirteen minutes of gardening before an "asthma attack" struck. (Ave actually does get asthma attacks, but when asked to participate in light-to-medium physical activity, she has "asthma attacks.")

"You do share DNA with her, so I'm sure you have some insight on this," I say, wheeling toward Avery. "Out of all the boys in school, even Mike Tossier, who looks like Ryan Gosling when you squint from a few paces away, why *Gideon*?"

I keep replaying it in my head—Gideon's arms around Ashley as he stared at her, charmed by her fake awkwardness as she laughed at his jokes, twirled her hair, sprayed her pheremonal glands or whatever—and berating myself with arrows and circles, like I'm examining a bad Super Bowl play.

"Is this what PTSD is like?" I whine.

In the middle of lighting the joint, Ruth gives me her patented *Shut up, you millennial twit* glare. I give her a hopeful *Pass that weed, brah!* smile. She firmly shakes her head, and I am secretly relieved. This is our usual dance.

"I just messed it all up," I mumble, turning back to the remaining bulbs.

"Oh, right, because before this, it absolutely looked like you guys were heading for homecoming court," deadpans Avery without looking up from her calc book.

"Shut your face, Wheezy."

Ruth clears her throat. "Well, *I* think"—she waits for both of us to give her due attention and respect—"*I* think it went better than you could've possibly imagined."

"You're kidding."

"Would you say it was 'unforgettable'?"

"No, because I'd like to forget it as quickly as possible."

"That wasn't my question."

"Actually, it was. You just have Alzheimer's."

Ruth doubles over and laughs so hard that the joint almost falls out of her mouth. She holds up her hand, signaling for us to give her a second to catch her breath. Sometimes I forget how old she is—I don't like to think about it. To be honest, these "being adjacent to mortality" moments are a bummer. I know it's strange to be friends with a seventy-three-year-old, but like most unlikely friendships, ours has kind of an origin story.

Back in freshman year social studies, I had to interview a senior citizen. All my grandparents had already shuffled off this mortal coil, and I didn't want to hit up the Melville Retirement Community because nursing homes creep me out. They're like drive-throughs for death.

The old lady across the highway, in the dilapidated house with the beautiful garden, seemed like the most convenient option. I didn't know her at all, but Dawn and everyone else on Leshin Lane seemed to think she was nuts—not just old lady nuts but ageless, mentally imbalanced, "she was like this when she was twenty" nuts.

I knocked on her door at around four thirty in the afternoon, figuring old people didn't go to bed until at least five. No response. I knocked again.

A voice, sounding surprisingly like a sprightly fifty-year-old's, snapped, "I'm not interested!"

"Um, I'm not selling anything."

She cracked the door just enough that the chain on the latch was taut. All I could see was a sliver of her face. "Go on, then."

Talking in that way you do when you know you have to sell somebody on your pitch in the next five seconds, I rushed: "I'm Scarlett Epstein your neighbor I have to do a project for school about studying American history on a personal level and I was wondering if you might have the time to——"

She shut the door in my face. I was flabbergasted. I knocked again, more insistently, and I heard her agitated footsteps slamming on the hardwood as she came back to the door. She swung it wide open so hard that the breeze blew my hair back.

Ruth was—is—what an old-fashioned novel would call a "handsome woman," almost six feet tall with thick gray-streaked hair piled on top of her head. She wore a crisp white short-sleeved shirt buttoned up all the way to the top, with the sleeves rolled like James Dean, and thick wool trousers. She didn't look like anyone else in town. In other words, she looked cool as hell.

"You Dawn Epstein's kid?"

"Um, yeah."

"I've seen her at Superfresh. Where's your dad at?"

"New York," I said, then for some reason felt compelled to add, "New wife."

Ruth looked at me for a minute, slouching in the doorway and sucking in her cheeks thoughtfully, her body language uncannily similar to the burnout kids at my school who hung out near the Stop sign just outside the school zone. Then she glanced conspiratorially around, even though it was just us in front of her empty house.

"You go to MHS?"

"Alas and alack, I do."

"Do you know where I could find some pot?"

My eyebrows shot up before I could control them.

"Pot like *pot*? Like marijuana?"

"No, pot like for tea. It's hard to get your hands on ceramic cookware," she deadpanned, looking exasperated. "Yeah. You know. Ganj. Whatever you're calling it now."

"I missed the last teen-slang standardization meeting, but I think we're calling it weed. You don't, like, have a person?"

"I think he graduated. I'll tell you, being retired and running out of your stash is kinda like having a peanut-butter-and-jelly sandwich without the peanut butter. Or the jelly. Just two dry pieces of bread."

Gamely attempting to roll with this, I agreed faintly, "That sounds like . . . not a good sandwich."

"Don't look so shocked. Getting high is just about the only good thing about being my age. Which is seventy-one, by the way. If there's some kind of crone age requirement for your project."

"That's a great age for my report, and you're not a crone," I told her firmly, trying and failing to feel out where all this was going.

She gasped like I insulted her. "Don't say that! I love being a crone.

"I don't know who came up with the stupid idea that we appreciate the little things, like domestic chores or sitting and watching the sun set like it's a goddamn Bourne movie. And you can use that in your report, by the way—if you help me out and track down a new dealer."

"Um, I don't think I know anybody."

She snorted derisively, reaching up to adjust the cockeyed tumble of gray hair looped up in a claw clip.

"What are you, sixteen?"

"Fifteen."

"In this town? Every other kid in your class probably has a hookup."

"I don't really—"

"Those are my terms, lady. Take it or leave it."

We sized each other up for a minute. She tilted her head up high, like she was challenging me. For a second I felt like Al Pacino in that scene in *The Godfather* where he shoots all those guys in that restaurant and then flees to Sicily and marries that girl who doesn't speak his language but has really nice breasts and then she gets blown up in a car.

Finally, I relented. "You're on."

Things I am extraordinarily good at locating: public restrooms, novels about hedonism and angst at exclusive private schools, quickly canceled cult TV shows, and free bagels. Controlled substances are not, and will never be, one of those things. Even picking up antibiotics for an ear infection at CVS makes me feel vaguely shifty and hyper-self-conscious, like a minor character on *The Wire*.

Fortunately, Ruth was right: Weed was as ubiquitous at school as folded brown-bag textbook covers with Drake lyrics scrawled on them. I located a hookup almost immediately when I sidled up to Mark Petruniak during Phys Ed and awkwardly said something like, "Hey, do you, like, I know you smoke, but do you happen to deal? I mean deal weed. Not, like, 'with issues.'"

To my relief, Mark laughed.

"Yeah, dude," he said super-nonchalantly, his eyelids drooping, and I caught a whiff that verified his honesty. "Hey, I didn't know you smoked."

"Well, sometimes," I lied modestly, basking in taking a well-liked guy from school by surprise. "You know. Not a lot."

(I smoked weed one time. It was at one of Ashley's parties. I freaked out, locked myself in the bathroom, and sobbed uncontrollably until Dylan Dinerstein drunkenly climbed in through the window to pee.)

After Phys Ed, I handed Mark a fifty, and he gave me a small plastic bag with some green stuff in it that could totally have been Astroturf and I wouldn't have known.

"Good shit," I said, as if I had a Ph.D. in Discerning Shit Quality.

"You should come to over my house and smoke sometime," Mark said casually.

"Yeah, definitely," I lied.

In retrospect, I felt fortunate that a number of small miracles had transpired: I managed to purchase marijuana without asking Mark what exact unit of measurement was in a dime bag, without getting arrested, and without being so nervous about potentially being arrested that I *Maria Full of Grace*-ed it home in my vagina.

I stopped by Ruth's house after school, just as the sun was setting, incredibly jittery from playing Pokémon with narcotics at school and hoping this stupid report would be worth all the anxiety.

She answered the door in the middle of my second knock.

"Yup."

"Hi. I got the thing. The stuff. You know." Beat. Nothing. "The stuff."

"Oh, right." A light clicked on behind her eyes. She looked mildly impressed but quashed it immediately. "Great, come on in."

The foyer was warm and cluttered in an eclectic, lived-in way. Best of all, there were books everywhere, mostly very old ones, lined up on one single long shelf that looped around the room endlessly, like literature dominoes. I glanced a little closer and saw that a lot of them were feminist theory—some I recognized from my own late-night smart-girl Googles, but others I didn't know.

"Dworkin is a loony tune." Ruth pulled one book down from the shelf. "You ever read her?"

I looked down at the book. *Intercourse*, read its stark cover. Nothing you'd find between *He's Just Not That Into You* and *Eat Pray Love* on Dawn's bookshelf. I shook my head.

"She makes reality TV look like *The Partridge Family*," Ruth said admiringly and handed the book to me. "Here. Keep it. I've read it."

"You haven't read, like, *all* of these, have you?"

"Yep."

"Whoa."

"Yeah, well. Thirty-four years teaching women's studies, you crack a book or two. Not that there's ever any right answer to this stuff." She shook her head with sort of a bemused smile. "It's amazing how the more you read, the less you know."

"I totally get what you mean," I said instantly. A second later, I realized I actually did. It was the first time I ever felt understood by a grown-up.

I tucked the book in my backpack, feeling a little bit like I'd just found the coolest informal library ever.

Ruth plucked the dime bag from my hand and brushed past me, heading into the kitchen, all Formica and peeling wallpaper. I followed behind. She lifted the lid of a porcelain sugar jar and placed the new plastic bag of weed inside it. She opened a junk drawer, pulled out some rolling papers, and started making a joint. Or a blunt. I'm still unclear on the difference, maybe the latter just isn't as polite at parties.

"You wanna start this Old Crone Report, then?" Ruth asked through gritted teeth, clenching the joint between them.

I nodded and took out my notebook.

"Okay." She breathed in, held it, frozen, then exhaled. A plume of smoke rose and twisted in front of us like a belly dancer. "You should know I'm not gonna give you any *Tuesdays with Morrie* bullshit."

I wrote that down.

"Life isn't a beautiful gift to treasure every moment of. It's shitty and unfair, and I'm not gonna give you any 'wisdom' on how to gracefully come to terms with life or death or anything."

I nodded.

She exhaled, visibly relaxed—her forehead wasn't tensed up anymore like it had been when I first knocked on her door—and shrugged.

"I could use a hand with the garden. If you want to come by a few days a week and help me out, you can pick my brain about when dinosaurs roamed Earth. How does that sound?"

"Yeah! Great."

"Good. Starting now. Can you show me how to do an emoji?"

She handed me a cracked iPhone with no case. She'd been texting with someone called "K.," flirtatiously bordering on straight-up smut.

I showed her how to access the emoji keyboard and handed it back. She vacillated between the wink face and the kiss-blowing face, then looked at me.

"Hello? Make yourself useful."

"Kiss, I think. Wink emoji is a little bit 'recently divorced dad.' Also," I said, "you spell *twerk* with an *e*."

She revised and hit Send, and I was glad to see the ghost of a smile on her face at my response.

"You want some bourbon?"

"I'm fifteen."

"What's your point?"

After one faded flower teacup full of bourbon, I was drunk. Ruth drank triple that and seemed totally fine, considering she was asking me what books I was reading in English class, whereas I was trying to focus my vision while wondering who I could possibly persuade via text to take my make-out virginity.

"What are you reading?"

"The Turn of the Screw."

"Good one. Classic. Sexual repression, ghosts—what's your teacher's name?"

"Mr. Radford."

"What's he like?"

"Uh, young." I thought. "Enthusiastic."

"You should do him!" She said it with the same tone of wholesome encouragement you'd use to say *You should do yoga!* or *You should visit Lake Placid!*

"What?!"

"Don't look at me like that. Every great writer has 'turned the screw' with a professor. Obviously it would be better if his balls hung a little lower, if he was older, more established, but . . ." She shrugged.

"Jesus Christ. Ew. Also, I'm not a—don't call me that."

"A what? A writer?"

I nodded.

"Why not?"

"It feels weird."

"It's supposed to feel weird. If it didn't, *that* would be a problem."

"Really?"

She nodded. "You want some more bourbon?"

Later that month, I finished my social studies assignment, which was honest to a fault (I got a B- and a *Please see me after class*, with "please" underlined thrice), but I stuck around to help with the garden, and Ruth and I have been friends ever since.

"You're really wasting your energy worrying about this," Ave informs me as she highlights some boring crap in her calc textbook. "Guys are like H&M tops to Ashley. Next week he'll be in the Goodwill bin, and my parents will yell at her for insisting she'd wear it forever and being so wasteful with their money."

I shake my head, gritting my teeth as I yank out the stubborn weeds congesting Ruth's zinnias. "It's because he's special and she knows it."

Ave makes a noise.

"Um, yes?"

"All I'm saying is, Ashley has horrible taste," Avery tentatively begins as I sweat all over Ruth's tea roses. "I mean, Kevin Rice? Hello?"

Ruth furrows her brow. "Who's Kevin Rice?"

"A tool," Ave and I say simultaneously.

"No. This is a tool." Ruth holds up her spade. "I don't know how either of you expect to get into good colleges if you can communicate only in street."

"Sorry, in *street*?" I say, aghast. "Tell me, then—what *is* the appropriate word?"

"Asshole," Ruth incants sagely and turns back to her petunias.

"Scarlett, maybe Ashley liking him is an indication that he sucks."

"Inconceivable."

"You only quote *The Princess Bride* when you're afraid I'm right."

"You're dismissed. The real question is, why would he even like her? Aside from looking like a Hollister model and getting perfect grades"—I wilt a little but continue—"her whole personality is put on."

Ruth shrugs, relighting the last of her J. "Sure. It's usually a phase. Girls figure out what boys want, they do it for a while, then they stop. Trust me, I used to see it every year when I was teaching."

"If she knows what boys want, I wish she'd tell me," Ave mumbles under her breath, then trills sardonically, "As my parents would say, we've both been 'blessed with our own gifts'! Here's mine"—she points to her head—"and here's hers." She pantomimes big boobs, then instantly looks guilty and stops talking. That's what happens whenever she rags on Ashley to me.

"I don't know." I sigh. "She's not entirely devoid of personality. She just fakes being all awkward and shy and nerdy. Maybe it's just what guys want now. Fake-awkward. She pretends to not know what she's doing when she's doing it."

Avery reluctantly nods.

"But that's what I mean," says Ruth. "You're genuine. There's no artifice in you."

"Often to your own detriment, bro," mumbles Ave. I glare at her. She looks away innocently.

"You're not the way you are and you don't talk the way you talk because you think that's what other people want from you." Ruth shrugs. "It's better. If you keep acting a certain way just because guys—or anyone—want you to, you'll regret it."

"It's like she's intentionally trying to make things—oh my GOD." I drop my rake, struck with a massive realization.

"Are you okay?" Ave asks, alarmed.

"I'm Anne Hathaway and she's Jennifer Lawrence!" I exclaim.

They both look at me like I'm insane.

"No, hear me out. Anne Hathaway is a celebrity. But she's a real person—like, nerdy and loud and enthusiastic and excited about stuff, and people think she's abrasive and they hate her.

"Whereas Jennifer Lawrence is, like . . . Anne Hathaway 2.0. I mean, she's the new and improved version. Her PR team COULD make her come off totally perfect. But she's designed precisely to *seem* like she's been programmed with similar 'real person' bugs—but in a super-appealing way, nothing too weird or unrelatable or abrasive. She sort of just seems to not give a shit. And everyone loves her because she's such a 'normal person,' even though she's not. You know?" I proclaim triumphantly. "Well, other than me."

There is a long pause.

Avery rolls her eyes and says, "You are just, like . . . an endless *font* of bullshit sometimes."

"Do those girls go to school with you?" Ruth asks, confused.

I'm about to reply when my phone signals I've received a text. I reach into the back of my shitty gardening jeans and pull it out. It's from Dawn, and it says: **Emergency. Come home right now.**

chapter six

AS I RUN UP THE STAIRS of our housing complex two by two, a gaggle of eleven-year-old boys start snapping those little dollar-store firecrackers in the parking lot. I flail. They laugh. Mission accomplished.

We're not poor, but after people at school—people whose families have refrigerators with water dispensers and ice makers built into them, or in-ground pools, or houses with an upstairs *and* a downstairs—started bitching about how the "middle class" is ignored by financial aid packages, I concluded that we are lower-lower middle class. Springsteen class, if you will, although I failed my written driver's test and therefore have avoided the highway jammed with broken heroes on a last-chance power drive.

I stick my keys in the door and slam hard against it—it's always jamming. This time it gives way easily, and I stumble inside.

Dawn's sprawled on the sofa still wearing her baby-blue house-keeping uniform. *Bridget Jones's Diary* is on in the background.

"What is it?" I'm gasping from the running.

She looks at me and starts sobbing words. All I can make out phonetically is something like, "I JUST, *MRAAAAAA*."

"Whoa, hey, holy shit." I drop my backpack on the floor and rush over to the sofa. She slides to the very end to make room for me, pushing herself with just her feet the way a kid would, her upper body remaining limp. A half-empty value pack of Twizzlers is tossed on the coffee table, the packaging ripped nearly in half. This is a bad sign, as Twizzlers are her sad food.

"What's wrong?" I ask, alarmed.

She continues to cry and shakes her head.

"Can you . . . try to tell me?"

These crying jags are frequent enough that I've developed an efficient strategy: half *Gilmore Girls*, half *Jeopardy!* I'll take Is It a Guy? for five hundred.

"Is it a guy?" I ask.

She nods, her face scrunching up and her eyes squeezing closed. It usually is, although occasionally it's a work thing, and, in one particularly scary white wine–fueled instance, an "I should have been a better mother" thing. This I could deal with.

"I thought we agreed to save emergency texts for actual dismemberment," I joke. She just looks at me. Her makeup has dripped down her face.

On our tiny TV, Bridget Jones bemoans how fat she is. In the two years since my dad left, I have watched a countless number of these movies with Dawn, but I will never get over how fucked up they are. I wrinkle my nose.

"I'll be honest with you; I'm not sure this is helping."

I mute the movie, and Dawn smiles, wan. She appears to have gotten a little calmer and wipes her eyes with the back of her hand, sniffling.

"So, what happened?"

"I went on a really good date." She sighs.

"From Match?"

"Yeah."

"And you're *crying*? I don't understand."

"God. It's just not gonna work out. You know?"

"Why? Is he married or something?" *Or a squatter? Or a twenty-five-year-old who said he's thirty-seven because he "likes cougars"? Or prone to saying "I know I'm not black, but . . ."?* Just a couple of her old chestnuts.

"No. I mean, not that I know of. I just . . . something's bound to be wrong with him, right? If he's single at this age?"

"Not necessarily! You're single at this age."

Dawn glares at me.

"I mean, your age! Okay, sorry, you're single at 'an' age."

"That's different. Single moms have a harder time."

Inside, I wince with guilt. Like, she could've just named me Baggage Joan Epstein and then at least we're all being honest.

"Well, I don't know! Maybe you're catching a break! I mean, finally, you know? You gotta climb up a mountain before you . . . I don't know. Something!"

As she watches me, clinging to every positive word I say like a life raft, I desperately try to come up with a home run. She is a big fan of inspirational quotes, saying "morning affirmations" in the mirror and all that stuff. To my dismay, as I'm grasping for something, her face begins to squinch up again. There's gotta be some beautiful, enlightening parable that'll make her feel better.

I blurt, "Did you see on the news the other day, that lady in Cincinnati who found a chicken fetus in her McNugget?"

"What?" Dawn recoils. "Sweetie, *ew*."

"Yeah, so, um, she ordered a six-piece McNugget, and she bit into one, and it made a weird noise, so she spit it out and saw that it was, like . . . a little unhatched chicken fetus. With, you know, breading or whatever."

Dawn is incredibly grossed out. I'd better cut to the chase.

"So, like—maybe that lady got a defective McNugget that one time. Or maybe even, like, a few other times. Probably not, because, I mean, it's unlikely, statistically speaking! But still so!"

I'm actually starting to work myself up with the disgusting pep talk at this point, but she still doesn't look like she's buying it. I soldier on.

"If that person really, really loved McNuggets, should a couple of chicken fetuses stop her from staying positive and getting right back into a McDonald's and taking a chance on more McNuggets?" I ask passionately.

"It probably . . . um, should . . ." she says faintly.

"No! It should NOT!" I'm totally into this now.

Dawn looks perplexed. "I mean, do they keep going to the same McDonald's? Because it seems like there are some major health violati—"

"Okay, I know, it's not a perfect metaphor. My point is, a couple of chicken fetuses shouldn't stop you from living your life! You see what I'm saying here?"

We both sit there sort of nodding encouragingly at each other for a couple of minutes like dashboard bobbleheads.

"I guess so." She gains traction, her face brightening. "Yeah. I guess. I mean, right?"

"Totally!"

"Yeah. You're right."

"I mean, McYolo, you know?"

"Absolutely. No, you're right. I just need to be positive."

Satisfied that I've diffused the worst of this crisis, I snatch a Twizzler.

"What's the guy's name?" I ask, gnawing on it.

She smiles tentatively. "Brian."

"What's he do?"

"Accountant."

"Has he called you yet?"

I have asked these questions so many times that I've developed a crisp and efficient delivery, like Mariska Hargitay on *Law & Order SVU* always asking the kid to point on the doll where the creepy uncle touched her.

"Yes. But I let it go to voice mail. I have to stay smart about it!

I don't want to seem like I like him too much," Dawn says sagely. She is really into all those dating mind-game books: *The Rules* and *Why Men Love Bitches* and *If You Do Something You Want to Do, You'll Literally Ruin Everything*.

I roll my eyes, like I usually do when she starts spewing this nonsense, and flick a Twizzler at her.

"Come on, who actually cares about that crap? That stupid 'Who cares less?!' death spiral is such a waste of time."

Dawn shakes her head.

"Nope. I didn't design it this way, but like I always tell you, the party with the least interest—"

"Has the most power," I finish along with her. "God, you've only been saying that since I was a zygote. Whatever. Disagree."

"I know it seems retro to you, but you'll see the light real soon," Dawn says confidently.

"I hope not," I groan. "It's so depressing."

She unmutes *Bridget Jones's Diary* right as Hugh Grant and his smirking face emerge from the elevator just as "R-E-S-P-E-C-T" starts playing.

Begrudgingly, I'm like, "Okay, that's a really legit sound cue. Good job, movie."

She smiles. Today's emotional crisis is out of the red zone.

"But please, please promise me you'll mute Colin Firth's 'just as you are' speech."

"I promise," Dawn lies.

I finally escape to my room.

Dawn's always been like this. Back in seventh grade, Avery had a slumber party. She, I, and a few other misfits from school that we had nothing else in common with got into sleeping bags in the Parkers' freezing-cold basement and watched *Mean Girls*. When Regina George's velour-tracksuited "not like a regular mom, I'm a cool mom" started handing out virgin daiquiris, I felt all six pairs of eyes swivel toward me, starting with Had Her Period on White Pants and Nobody Told Her Leslie and ending with Legitimately Mentally Slow Jenna.

And those are just my *friends'* reactions. Last year at the Drama Club fall potluck dinner, Dawn rushed in, tugging down the hem of her electric-blue bandage dress, with boxed Entenmann's cookies she tossed hastily on the table with the other moms' homemade casseroles and pies.

"Who's the old skank?" Ashley asked Natalia, not quietly (she probably thinks sotto voce is a type of coffee), knowing perfectly well that the old skank was my mom.

Later, predictably, they sang "Take Me or Leave Me" from *Rent* as both sets of parents filmed it from opposite sides of the audience, because to get only one angle would have been a huge social injustice.

At worst, Dawn and I don't get along. At best, we confuse each other. Like, she's in a zillion Meetup groups that all have some misleading title like "Melville Museumgoers" but are just a cover for a bunch of women drinking pinot grigio in someone's den and talking about how shitty their kids and ex-husbands are. She comes home, and I ask her something pointed like "Did you check out the Goya exhibit?" and she replies distantly, "I had a really good share today." Then she pours white wine over some ice cubes, goes into her bedroom, shuts the door, and listens to one Macy Gray song on repeat.

Dawn thinks I should open up and be more receptive to groups. I remind her that history rarely reflects well on groups of people who bond and get carried away. "You're more like your father every minute" is her muttered reply. Sometimes I get the feeling she wants to squash the Dad half of me like it's a cockroach. She even tried to get me to use her maiden name for a hyphenated surname. I said the only way on Earth I'd do that is if her maiden name was Barr, which it is not.

Her most blatant attempt to "connect" with me came in the form of a trip to Disney World. We drove down, sharing a motel bed on the way. But my mother omitted one important piece of information, which was that we could only afford the vacation in the first place because some timeshare was having a promotion. In exchange for the discount rate, we had to sit through a three-hour tour of available units and get the skinny on why going in on a three-bedroom condo in Fort Lauderdale was the Best! Decision! Ever!

I knew I'd have to distract Dawn from the details of the pitch because she's one of those people who always says "Yes!" when canvassers in New York stop us and ask if we care about starving children or if we get our hair cut. Even that time it made us twenty minutes late to see her favorite musical, which obviously is *Rent*.

To preoccupy her, I started whispering stories about the employees as they showed us around: "Milania and Alex commiserated about what a waste college was last week at TGI Fridays and wound up sleeping together even though he has a girlfriend.

"Devin who just offered us Diet Cokes obviously wanted to be an actor, and every time some retiree stops his pitch mid-sentence to ask a question, he hopes that they'll request the 'ABC' monologue from *Glengarry Glen Ross*, but of course it never happens."

She stared at me.

"Don't tell me you don't remember," she said.

"Remember what?"

"Your dad used to do that."

I'd forgotten, but it came back to me in bits and pieces as soon as she said it. He'd tell us voyeuristic tales of the people in front of us at the DMV and make up backstories about the waitresses to keep us entertained while we waited to be seated at Perkins. At least, he'd do that in the rare instances he wasn't locked in his bedroom working on his novel.

A lot of my memories from when I was little revolve around that closed door and Dawn taking me to get Dairy Queen or putting on a really inappropriate movie like *Basic Instinct* or *Fatal Attraction* to distract me. We had even less money than we have now, so it made no sense to me when Dawn would say, "Daddy's working." I get it now that I'm older, but sometimes I worry, like a big old Lifetime movie child-of-divorce cliché, how much I had to do with him leaving. If I'm part of what he wanted to upgrade from.

Dawn was waiting for me to say if I remembered or not. But it's not a time I like thinking about.

"Look." I pointed to a pretty girl at the wheel of a Lexus, texting frantically. "Alex's girlfriend just found out she's pregnant."

I check my phone. It's eight twenty. We'd be well into the episode by now. I feel like I'm in detox. I decide to call my stepmom, Kira, who is an excellent person to answer what I want to ask because she's written about pop culture for basically every highbrow magazine and blog on the planet.

"Hello, Scarlett!" Her lilting English accent is like aural Vicodin.

"Hey. Why do people like Jennifer Lawrence so much?"

"Why do you ask?"

"Because I don't think I like her, but if I tell any other American, I'm worried my citizenship will be revoked."

Kira laughs, and I hear my baby half sister, Matilda, giggle, probably from Kira's lap.

"Well, what don't you like about her?"

I twist my mouth into a frown at the wall, struggling to find the words. I always want to be especially articulate for Kira.

"It's like . . . she has such a good PR team that she knows she should pretend to have no PR team. Or she's so overly calculated that she knows she should pretend to be uncalculated."

"First of all, Scarlett," says Kira, with a smile in her voice, "if you put this much thought into school, you'd be the valedictorian."

"But seriously . . . why do people respond to that?"

There was a thoughtful pause on the other end. Then she finally said, "I'd wager people like looking at how little effort she puts into, say, late-night shows. They identify with it. It makes them feel like they can be lazy, and it'll come off like effortless charm. Does that help at all?"

"Yeah, thanks."

"What's this for?"

"No reason," I mumble.

She has to go shortly after, profusely apologizing because she and my dad are late for a dinner party.

Dawn's acted even more psycho since Dad married Kira, a gorgeous black Englishwoman who looks immaculate in Google image search, even as far back as page fifteen of the search results. She's thirty, smart, and pedigreed as hell—she got six figures for her debut novel, which came out last year. She is one of those women who doesn't eat any bread at restaurants but would never judge you for eating it. Whereas Dawn's and my motto is basically "Can we get some more bread for the table?" in Latin. It makes way more sense for Dad to be married to Kira. I asked him once why he married my mom. He thought about it for a minute, then finally said, "She was fun."

Not lately. Dawn hates when I geek out with Kira over books—the very first time we met, we immediately discovered our shared love of *The Secret History*. And Dawn *really* hated, before they got married and Kira's book came out, how impressed and flattered I was that Kira used to talk to me about the editing process like I was a grown-up, an actual writer.

Now that the *Lycanthrope* cast photo is gone, a photo of Matilda is the only one wedged in the rusty outside door of my locker. She's like the most perfect baby ever, good-natured and smiley with deep dimples, like a babyGap model. She may be my half sister, but she'll grow up in a totally different world— even her name evokes intellect and specialness—which I try not to think about too much or I get jealous. It's one thing to be jealous of Ashley Parker but a whole other thing to be jealous of a prehuman who doesn't even know what her own feet are.

They live in a gorgeous, airy loft in Brooklyn. It makes sense with Matilda and Kira's book and everything that they don't really have much time to invite me over and why my dad doesn't call as much as he used to. He's probably really stressed out— I'm a lot like him, so I can tell. Last year I tried to persuade Dawn to let me move in with them, and she flipped out. *If I'm so horrible and he's so great, why doesn't he ever come to see you? Why aren't his checks ever on time?*

It doesn't have anything to do with me. She just doesn't want to live alone. And more than that, she doesn't want Kira and my dad to win.

I try my best to go to New York all the time. Avery and I

go see Upright Citizens Brigade, then run to catch the last New Jersey Transit express from Penn Station back to Melville at one A.M. While we're sitting on the train and Ave's napping next to me, I look out the window at the pinpricks of twinkling lights receding in the darkness and think about living in New York. It's like the closest thing to a John St. Clair show there is in real life, where everybody's like my dad and Kira—smart and articulate and creative—and I'd never feel alone.

When I started writing fics, they were mostly about Connor and Becca. They're not the most popular pairing—one-third of the Gillian love triangle, and Gillian's sarcastic plus-size best friend—so it took me a while to figure out why people liked my fanfics as much as they did. I guess I'm funny, something I seem to be the last to know about. I never thought about it until last year at the mall when I made this girl pee her pants. I didn't know her that well—Avery met her in their accelerated-genius Princeton math class and invited her along without asking me.

I don't even remember what I said to make her laugh so hard; I just remember going on compulsively for, like, five minutes until she was squeezing her legs crossed in front of the clearance rack in Wet Seal and breathlessly begging me to stop. It's mostly useless—a party trick, like being double-jointed. No decent college would accept someone with a 2.9 GPA just because she once made some girl have to run to the food court bathroom and stick her Seven7 jeans under the hand dryer.

Scarface: What'd I miss?

xLoupxGaroux: WELL. We've been talking about doing one last fic challenge. It didn't really end. And the fix-its are okay, but they're getting hammered. Every time someone uses the canon characters, people flip out on them about whatever ending they made up.

Scarface: What about the next matriculating class at Pembrooke?

xLoupxGaroux: Like, a number of years later, you mean?

Scarface: Yeah. All OFCs and OMCs. Blank slate, same world, same rules.

WillianShipper2000: ugh idk if i even WANT to make up my own, we could just switch to a diff show

xLoupxGaroux: TRAITOR

DavidaTheDeadly: actually . . . scarface, that's not a bad idea.

Scarface: Willian, think about it: You can write your *own* couple to ship! And Loup, you're always complaining there's too much het fic. This would be a make-your-own.

xLoupxGaroux: OK. Hold up.

Loup is our de facto snarky leader. He doesn't suffer fools, but his deepest, darkest secret is that he's essentially a nice person. Otherwise he'd never tolerate Willian's basicness—the *Lycanthrope* fandom can be snobby about that stuff.

> **xLoupxGaroux: There's got to be a checks-and-balances system . . . one of us writes a bunch of installments, and the rest of us give feedback. Because when left unchecked, OFCs can be really goddamn irritating.**
>
> **DavidaTheDeadly: calm down dude, i think we've all proven we're above mary sues here.**
>
> **DavidaTheDeadly: alright. so. installments?**

I admit, my motive here is to keep us all together as long as possible. But I think theirs is too. Even if they don't say it.

> **DavidaTheDeadly: scarface, it was your idea, so you first.**
>
> **Scarface: Haha. Goddammit. OK.**
>
> **xLoupxGaroux: Are you gonna cry again?**
>
> **Scarface: Shut up.**
>
> **xLoupxGaroux: Tell you what. If you kick us off with some original characters—who are not annoying—we can take it from there.**
>
> **Scarface: Deal.**

If this is what it takes to keep it going, fine. I almost don't want to mess with werewolves—John made them so much his own that if I touch them, I may as well be writing yet another Connor/Becca fic. I still feel a little weird about inventing people. They're usually unrealistically perfect or tortured or something. If I write them wrong, all my credibility in the community will be shot. Writing *Lycanthrope* fic was easier because I knew those characters just as well as I know Avery, or Ruth, or—oh.

The Ordinaria
Part 1
submitted by scarface_epstein

Shit, shit, shit, and furthermore, goddamn it.

Gideon was hoping that his school wouldn't be the first. But it was, of course. Pembrooke Academy was one of the best—and most expensive—private high schools in the country. If they started it at some random public school, it would be like opening a Rolls dealership in Trenton. Gideon knew this because he'd heard his father snap, "Are you kidding me? It would be like opening a Rolls dealership in Trenton," to Steve Mullen on the phone in his home office last night.

Gideon paused in the middle of the hallway and pressed his ear to the door. His father, CEO of Ordinaria Inc., was talking to his four advisers: Steve Mullen, his assistant Steve

J., *his* assistant Steve P., and Don.

"I agree," said Steve Mullen, the most levelheaded of the bunch. "We sank all this money into a new product for this whole 'get the teens' campaign, so why not place them with the affluent and horny? We'll make our money back in five seconds flat. I vote Exeter, Andover, Deerfield, and Pembrooke."

"Yeah, start elite, build some buzz," Steve P. said.

"It certainly worked for Facebook," Don chirped.

"Shut up, Don," said Steve P., because Don was his assistant.

"All due respect, Mitch, would that cause any problems with your son?" asked Steve Mullen, the only Steve who could get away with that question because he'd lost a teenage daughter years before, and even Gideon's dad still walked on eggshells around the topic.

"You mean Gideon?" (His father said this as if Gideon was not an only child.) "How so?"

"Well, all due respect, you're dumping fifteen female teenage sex robots into his senior class. That might . . . have some kind of effect on his school."

Gideon could practically hear his dad roll his eyes through the door.

"Steve, you've met my son. He should *thank* me."

* * *

The first day of school was always a mixed blessing, Gideon thought as he walked across the campus with a stream of other students in identical starchy blazers and awkward ties.

For one thing, he didn't have a girlfriend. You're not incredibly popular with girls when your father is considered the most destructive force for women's body image since Barbie. As for guys, he always suspected—rightly—that any male student who asked if he wanted to play some lacrosse or go to the movies later was trying to befriend him only for an Ordinaria discount. (Which was illegal anyway, unless they went through their dads. Can't have forty-year-old Ordinarias making out with fourteen-year-old boys in the quad.)

On the bright side, during the school year Gideon didn't have to hear his dad scream at a Breast Crafter that a nipple was too large. Most things were preferable to that, including but not limited to dancing in battery acid.

Gideon was seventeen, and since the day he'd been born, he'd watched his father build his empire, heard him endlessly pitching to donors when Ordinaria Inc. was just a start-up. Ten years of massive success later, and Gideon could recite the hard sell by heart.

[To billionaire.] *Listen. All it takes is one down payment and a very reasonable time line to pay the balance, and you'll be happy for the rest of your life. That's the* only thing *this product is wired for. They won't turn down tickets to the Stones because they're too tired. They won't drink three glasses of white wine and ignore you. They're not cranky. They're not complicated. They're not . . .* [dramatic pause, air of horror] *real.*

It worked massively well. *Forbes*-well. The Maclaines were

nationally, legendarily wealthy. And to be honest, after going through what he was sure was one of the stranger puberties in history, Gideon was totally used to them. Blasé, even. At this point he sort of saw them as can openers with cleavage.

So they decided to skew younger. Who cares?

* * *

The fact that Dean Arnolds appeared visibly psyched and Dean Jacobs looked incredibly depressed was an immediate giveaway. The five hundred students assembled in Maclaine Hall immediately started whispering and smacking one another on the shoulder. Most of them knew what was coming. The Internet's good like that. Some of them didn't dare hope for it. Others had sworn up and down that if it happened, they'd transfer to the local public school, zombie teachers and lackluster facilities be damned.

"We have an announcement—" Dean Jacobs began.

"We have a fantastic announcement." Dean Arnolds beamed.

Dean Jacobs glared at him, and he wilted just a bit as she continued.

"We are thrilled to announce," Dean Jacobs unconvincingly lied, "that we've been chosen as one of the first secondary institutions to host Miss Ordinarias."

Immediately, enough male students' eyes lit up that you could see it from space, with the exception of a bored handful who wondered, *God, where are the male ones already?* The girls were sullen, scuffing their penny loafers against the hardwood floor. One girl right next to Gideon began to sob.

"As you may know," Dean Jacobs continued, her face increasingly deadening, "while Ordinarias are primarily marketed to ages thirty-five to sixty, Miss Ordinarias are designed to appeal to the eighteen-to-twenty-five demographic."

A collective slap as two hundred high fives were given.

"*Attention!*" snapped Dean Jacobs, stomping her designer heel once, hard.

Everyone was quiet again.

"This is still Pembrooke, and I fully expect every one of you to act accordingly," she barked. Underneath, her defeat was audible.

"Oh, lighten up, Shelly!" said Dean Arnolds, slapping her on the fragile back so heartily that she stumbled forward. She tugged the hem of her suit back in place and glared daggers at him. He didn't care.

"I hope you all know who to thank for this," bellowed Dean Arnolds cheerfully. "Because his son is among you. Right here . . . in . . . this . . . room. Gideon Maclaine, where are you?"

Then 999 eyes (those of all five hundred students, including Kenny Adaire, who'd lost an eye last summer in a freak racquetball accident) flaring with all sorts of emotions turned toward Gideon at once.

For a second you could hear a pin drop, if anybody had a pin. But nobody had a pin, so the only thing plummeting was Dean Jacobs's patience.

The sobbing girl broke the silence by crying harder while

glaring at Gideon, which was terrible. Whenever he saw a girl crying, even a random one in the quad, he felt weirdly guilty, like he was somehow responsible. This time, he actually *was* responsible.

"Son of Mitchell Maclaine," Dean Arnolds continued. Gideon felt like he was in the Bible. "CEO of Ordinaria Inc., who's an entrepreneur, an innovator, and a massive donor I'm sure we're *all* incredibly grateful for."

That last bit was pointed, clearly addressed to the girls: *Remember the name of this hall. Remember who funded your equestrian classes. Where you should have learned to REIN IT IN.*

* * *

The delivery was the following Thursday. It was the first day in Pembrooke history that nobody, not even the stoners, cut class—but attendance didn't matter because class was shot to hell. Students and teachers alike gathered by the window to watch as the Ordinaria Inc. truck pulled around the school's cul-de-sac. Gideon was the only one in SAT Prep who didn't leap up to watch the action—even Mrs. Greer, who was ancient and seemed surprised by nothing, was straining at the window like the rest of them.

Gideon didn't have to run to the window because he had seen it a million times. He knew the deal. Right on cue, all the guys in class sighed and groaned with disappointment when the Ordinarias weren't pulled out of the truck in clear Barbie-like casing, naked and on display.

It was marginally classier than that. Each one came in a long white rectangular container—sort of a coffin/pastry-box hybrid. As per usual, overlaid on a big pink lipstick kiss print, in the company's iconic cursive font, was AUTHENTIC PRODUCT, ORDINARIA INC. On each of these, though, was a hastily stuck-on label in standard type instead: MISS ORDINARIA—TEST PRODUCT.

"You think they're naked in there, bro?" Dylan Dinerstein asked Paul Watts, because of course.

"No," Gideon said reflexively. Everyone looked at him. He bit his tongue.

Homely, sweet Lisa Lerner turned to him, her cowlike eyes enormous and pleading.

"They're gonna be nice, right?" she asked.

It was at this moment that Gideon remembered when his father had once described *2001: A Space Odyssey* as a slapstick comedy.

"Yeah, um. Of course they will," he said.

* * *

Even Gideon had been wondering exactly how much would be different from the Ordinaria proper model, with which he was very well acquainted—a beautiful thirty-to-fifty-year-old ersatz woman, brightened, less weary, and not as caustic as a human female of her age. Sometimes they were so lifelike it was uncanny. But Gideon could always tell by their eyes, the one feature that had frustrated his father to no end. No matter how many new developers or how much money he threw at it, there was something impossible to get just right.

The classroom door swung open, and Gideon noticed the absence of the familiar whirring noise that Ordinarias made. But there in the doorway was a Miss Ordinaria.

The class fell silent, but their expressions were united: *Holy shit.*

Gideon's breath caught in his throat very unexpectedly. She was gorgeous, in a totally different way than the Ordinarias Gideon had grown up with. Her skin was glowing but still seemed real; her face was just unique enough to pass for a real girl's. She had a little bit of (improbably becoming) rosacea. She was . . . God, just *really sexy*. As soon as the thought crossed his mind, he was furious with himself, like his father had just scored a point.

She came in and stood at the front of the room, wearing a slightly outdated tank top and jeans, but she was all the more beautiful for it. The girls glared.

"What's . . . um . . . what's your name, sweetheart?" asked Mrs. Greer, who barely knew how to use a smartphone and was trembling ever so slightly.

"Hi, I'm Ashbot." She faced the class and waved a little, tossed her red hair. "I'm here to get an education, I guess, or whatever."

"I'd like to educate her so hard she can't walk tomorrow," mumbled Chris Thompson, and two boys behind Gideon snickered.

"Have a seat, dear." Mrs. Greer was so freaked out that she was almost imploring Ashbot.

She whirred softly down the third row of desks, toward Gideon's, and he got a whiff of a super-girlie Bath and Body Works perfume that must have scored high on the Preferred Scent of Eighteen-to-Twenty-Five-Year-Old Men Test. Gideon's demographic. *They were dead on*, he thought, stupefied.

She stopped at his desk and stood over him, her green eyes wide and loving. The whole class stared.

"Hey, Gideon," she said. His name sounded very personal in her mouth. He swallowed hard.

Then, smiling, she cooed, "I'm your eighteenth birthday present."

* * *

"I need to talk to you!"

To his credit, this was the first time that Gideon had dramatically stormed into the Ordinaria Inc. boardroom. He had disregarded the secretaries' protests but tried his best not to be a huge dick about it.

His father was mid-meeting, in one of the many that made up his day. Seventeen men and two women sat around a long conference table. They all looked up when Gideon burst in.

"I'm not sure if you've noticed, but I'm busy right now," his father replied, gritting his teeth, obviously surprised by his son's gall.

Gideon ran out of steam and complied, just one of the latest series of compliances that made up his whole life. He seemed to be getting closer and closer to asserting himself but never quite going the distance.

He sat in the waiting room until his dad came out, then stood up and walked toward him with resigned determination, like someone ready to argue with a doctor about a loved one's fatal prognosis.

"So you got my gift," said his dad.

"Yeah. In front of my whole class. This is bullshit, Dad. You need to get me out of it," Gideon snapped, turning bright red.

"I thought you'd be happy."

"You're not doing this for me; you're doing this so I can be the, like . . . unofficial ambassador of integration. The first one to actually date it. The least you could do is be honest."

His dad shrugged. "Gid, you've got to lose it sometime."

Gideon winced. The secretaries studiously pretended not to hear.

"You could stand to be a little more appreciative, you know. She's designed especially for you. My team and I pretty rigorously studied a couple of years' worth of your, uh, browser history—"

"You. Are. Not. Saying. This. To. Me."

"She's about half a mil on the market. Rent her out if you want. Hell, you could sell her on eBay and buy a house on Nantucket with that kind of money."

"I don't give two shits about Nantucket," snapped Gideon.

"The Cape, then." His dad looked around, exasperated. "I have to get back in there. We can talk more about this at home, if you really want to."

This was his father's way of saying *End of discussion*.

Gideon slowly closed his eyes and took a very, very deep breath. "So you're telling me it's done."

Then his dad did something incredibly strange. For the first time in a decade or so, he reached out and tousled Gideon's hair. Gideon was so taken aback that he didn't have the reflex to smack his hand away.

His dad looked at him, bemused, and chuckled as he headed back to the boardroom.

"Oh, kid. Is it ever done."

* * *

Later that week, Ashbot was pouting. It seemed to be her default.

"Are you gonna touch my boobs soon?"

"No," Gideon said, for the seventeenth time that day. He was at his locker, and she was leaning up against the one next to his—a locker whose male freshman owner was standing awkwardly next to them, gawking too hard to ask her to move.

"Why?"

"I, um, I can't. I just can't."

Ashbot sighed.

She had not left his side since the day she arrived at school. Partly because she was absorbing how Gideon walked, talked, and seemed to think, in order to better simulate a real teenager. Gideon had seen enough newly manufactured Ordinarias following his mom around the grocery store and asking inane questions to know that much.

He just wished Ashbot's hair didn't smell so good.

"So after school, are we, like, gonna go somewhere or something or whatever, yo?" she asked.

Ashbot's language had been programmed with research adults had done on how teenagers spoke. It was bad.

"Ashbot." He tried to sound kind, but firm. "Nobody at this school talks like that."

She tilted her head, listening intently.

Then, guilelessly, she asked, "How do they talk?"

He thought about it.

"Like . . . God, I don't know. Not like in the movies. I know that isn't very helpful," he said apologetically.

Ashbot nodded understandingly. "Word."

xLoupxGaroux: Rolling with the robot subplot! Ho-LEE-Shit. Ballsy move. But I think you actually made it semi-interesting. Solid work.

WillianShipper2000: agree!!

xLoupxGaroux: I could use some more hot guys. But, yeah, some simmering (boring hetero) sexual subtext in here . . . Get thee to a nunnery, Scarface.

WillianShipper2000: wait y should she be a nun??

xLoupxGaroux: SMALL FRY. Google it.

WillianShipper2000: don't call me a fry

DavidaTheDeadly: guys!!!!

xLoupxGaroux: Hiiiiiii!

DavidaTheDeadly: scarface, this is . . . unsurprisingly . . . a weird story. but i'm into it! at the very least, it's making my work day go a little quicker.

xLoupxGaroux: Ehh . . . I dunno how much robot I'm down for at this point.

DavidaTheDeadly: but think about where John would take something like this! Ashbot would totally transcend her origins. look at Davida, she was a werewolf raised in loup garou culture, but she learned how to be a girl.

I roll my eyes.

DavidaTheDeadly: in any case, I am into it. if you need a beta reader LMK. More pls.

WillianShipper2000: me too!

xLoupxGaroux: Agreed. Featuring more hot guys. And a shirtless Gideon please.

DavidaTheDeadly: Ditto.

WillianShipper2000: ditto.

Ditto.

chapter seven

MR. RADFORD PASSES OUR TESTS back and minutely shakes his head at me as he slides mine onto the table. Thirty-seven. A disgruntled noise comes from behind me. Gideon's glaring at his test. Also thirty-seven. He glances at me, and when I catch him looking, he looks away. Then when he thinks I'm not paying attention, he looks at me again.

When the bell rings, he catches up to me by the door.

"Hey!"

I stop, my heart pounding hard enough to shake my brain. Even before we got our tests back, for some reason, I could feel him looking at me the whole period, boring holes in the back right side of my head. And it's not a good feeling, it's that nauseous fight-or-flight feeling I get when I see Ashley and Natalia looking either near me or at me and whispering something and laughing. But that's not fair, because *he's* the one who did something wrong.

"Maybe you shouldn't have cheated on me," I blurt. "Oh. Ha, cheated *off* me. Is what I meant."

He stares.

"Because, like, I didn't do the reading," I add.

"Yeah, I got that." He waves the test he's still holding.

"Well. I never promised you a rose garden. So. Okay. Um." I awkwardly slip by under his armpit and speed-walk to my locker, wishing for the first time that I'd done the reading and his A+ on the test had helped him get into Dartmouth. Then he'd owe me one. Then . . . that is the end of the plan, really. I'm so lost in fantasies that I don't notice him following me to my locker.

"Scarlett, hold up."

My name coming out of his mouth so casually gives me a head rush, like emotional brain freeze. He pauses in front of my locker, running his hand through his hair.

"I was kind of a dick the other day, I know. But it was weird, what you said. I do have friends."

"What?" It takes me a second before I realize that he's talking about my verbal brain fart from the other day.

"I mean, they don't go here. I know that sounds fake, like how girls are like"—he does a girl voice—"'I have a boyfriend, but he doesn't go here,' and actually they're just making it up. But I'm not."

"Okay," I say.

He shifts, irritated. "Don't just say okay if you still don't believe me."

"I do believe you!" I mean it.

"I have friends," he says again, then makes a face that's like *Oh shit, the more I say that, the faker it sounds.* At that moment, I am even more positive that Gideon and I have a lot in common. I feel protective, like I need to rescue him.

"Um, so why did you copy off me in the first place?" I strike a come-hither pose I see Dawn use with her boyfriends—hip jutted out, head cocked to the side, back arched a little more than is natural. It feels, and probably looks, quite strange.

"I thought you were good in English. I always see you reading."

He has noticed me. Reading. But still. Noticed me!

"Have you ever seen me reading any books on the English syllabus?"

He shakes his head. I raise my eyebrows, and he smiles a tiny bit, and I might actually die right here.

"Only *Lycanthrope* graphic novels. Which are you on?"

"Number fifty-five," I manage.

"Oh, right before Sam Kieth starts illustrating. He's awesome. Do you know him?"

I shake my head.

"Well, you'll see. I bet you'll like him a lot."

I nod emphatically like seventeen times in a row. "Yeah! Yeah, that sounds cool; I'll check it out."

"So you're pretty bummed about the show?"

"I mean, yeah, sure, I thought it was good, didn't you?" I barely recognize the faux-casual voice coming out of my mouth. (So this is how it happens. This is how girls change for boys.

I am simultaneously annoyed at myself and mildly amazed that I have the ability.)

He nods.

"How come you didn't want to talk to me about it the other day?" I ask.

"I didn't not want to; you just caught me off guard. I mean, we haven't talked in years. . . ."

I can feel the conversation heading south, but I can't stop myself. "Weird. Because I saw someone else come up to you right after that, and I don't think she's spoken to you *ever,* and you seemed pretty okay with it."

He looks freaked out. "What are you talking about?"

From down the hall, a pair of padded boobs turns toward us and actually seems to *aim*, like they're preparing to fire stealth missiles. The girls around her, dressed almost identically with slight variations, are either staring at me or at their phones.

Ashley says something to Natalia, smirking, and walks toward us. I'm suddenly conscious of what I'm wearing: a T-shirt, baggy jeans, a headband I borrowed from Dawn's Blair Waldorf–inspired headpiece collection hastily pushed over my two-day-unwashed hair.

When Ashley draws close enough, she leaps into Gideon's arms and curls up. She is like the opposite of those animals who puff up to scare away predators; she shrinks herself into something as delicate and girly and palatable as possible to snag her prey. My stomach starts to burn. Crushes are so stupidly physical sometimes, like colds.

"Hiiii-yyyyyyyyyeeeeeeee," she croaks, torturing out the salutation into seven million syllables, then slides down him like a pole and looks at me. "Hey, Divider!"

"Hi."

She turns to Gideon. "Did I ever tell you this? Sophomore year I was driving to a party, and I saw Scarlett on Route 9 by the Walmart, dancing on the divider."

(This is what actually happened: Dawn called me crying after some guy dumped her in the parking lot of Stop-n-Fresh. I had to take the public bus from the stop on our street to that strip mall that lets out on the highway, and then was running—*not* dancing—down the divider toward the parking lot to physically drag her away from a lonely pink-drink bender at a shitty bar. Ashley was making an unfortunately timed turn into the parking lot when she saw me "dancing." The good news is that I now know the stories behind every tattoo inked on some dude named "McG.")

"I wasn't dancing," I say, for the twentieth time, bracing myself as I feel her slowly pulling the guillotine up.

"Oh, hey!" Her sea-green eyes sparkle maliciously. "Can you tell your mom she did *such* a good job cleaning our bathroom?"

My head rolls down the hall.

She laughs, tinkly like a fairy's cough. "Sorry, I'm *so* random, it's just that we've had so many housekeepers, but she's really above average. She even speaks English!"

"It's true!" I say.

"Maybe the hotel staff in Cabo can pick up some tips from her when we're there!"

I'm confused. "In . . . Cabo?"

"Yeah, she better have her bag packed! She——" Her face drops. "Oh my God, I'm sooooo sorry. My mom organizes this trip to Cabo every year for people who live in the Manor and have kids in Drama Club . . . but you guys don't live in the Manor, do you?"

"Sure don't!"

Melville Manor is not as rich as it sounds, but Dawn would call it comfortable, which is her euphemism for "richer than us." Almost all the popular girls at school live there, two minutes apart, and throw house parties every weekend. Every year since 2012, when Megan Mullen died in a car accident biking home from one of those parties, local cops have staged a graphic bike-car accident on the football field for us all to internalize. Last year, Natalia Zacoum lay on the five-yard line in front of a Ford Taurus, half-on and half-off a Schwinn, smeared with fake blood. All the popular girls cried. Jessicarose Fallon passed out. It was hilarious.

"Sorry, ugh, I'm *sooooo* awkward," she says, leaning casually against Gideon's shoulder as if she is too top-heavy to support herself on her own, and asks him, "Are you going to the Halloween dance?"

He shrugs.

"I was on the decorations committee. So much drama, I can't even." (From overhearing snippets of conversation since freshman year, it seems that Ashley has a chronic condition of not being able to even.)

He glances down at her, then looks away and rolls his eyes in sort of a fond way, with an enigmatic little laugh. She links her arm through his and starts pulling him away from me like a determined little tugboat wearing Tory Burch flats. He turns back, once, and points at me.

"Hey. Don't forget. Sam Kieth."

"I wo—"

"You're such a dork," Ashley tells him sweetly, stepping on my words.

"*You're* a dork," he teases her back, their flirting irritatingly effortless. They start walking away, linking up with a bunch of other popular kids, Gideon looking irritatingly at home with them.

But then he turns around and looks back at me one more time.

chapter eight

The Ordinaria
Part 2
Submitted by Scarface_Epstein

It was week four of the Miss Ordinaria control test at Pembrooke. Fifteen beautiful teenage robots walking around in the school uniform, pausing and just standing in the dark common room every night and reactivating when the students came in, had become normal-ish. More than that, it was beginning to feel less like a crazy science experiment than a mass craving for the latest smartphone—exactly what Gideon's dad had hoped for.

It started with the douche-bags. Jason Tous, one particularly obnoxious senior whose parents were massively generous supporters of an unpopular political party—and, worse, he wore a really stupid jacket—had been boasting for weeks.

"My parents say if I get a twenty-three hundred on my SATs, I can get a down payment for one of those. Whichever one I want. Maybe even a custom model."

The other guys looked insanely jealous. Then they all glanced in what they thought was a subtle way over at Gideon. He knew they were thinking: *That quiet loser has what we all want, and he doesn't even care.*

Gideon pretended he didn't see them and secretly checked his phone under his desk.

Inbox (1)

It was from an address he didn't recognize: anonymous@ Pembrooke.edu. This wasn't the typical format of student e-mail addresses. Gideon's was GMaclaine@Pembrooke.edu.

He opened it. It read:

You're not what you think you are.

That was it. End of e-mail. Gideon read it again and still couldn't make anything of it.

He glanced around the room to see if someone was messing with him. Mr. Reed stood at the blackboard, two or three kids everyone hated listening intently, the rest zoning out, and Jason Tous talking quietly about a freshman's weird vagina. Just calculus as usual.

* * *

Eventually Gideon started trying to dodge Ashbot, but she was tough to lose, considering she was designed to stay only a certain distance from him unless he pressed a tiny sensor on the small of her back. And he was not going anywhere near the small of her back. Not that he wasn't tempted.

One afternoon, as she followed him to AP Chemistry, it occurred to him that the mysterious e-mail might have something to do with her—maybe someone in Ashbot's past was trying to intimidate him. Then again, it would mean that his dad had lied, that Ashbot wasn't actually custom-made for Gideon and fresh out of the box. He had to admit: It wasn't implausible, considering his dad was full of shit regularly.

But—ugh, did he have to ask her? It was so awkward. Finally he bit the bullet. As the late bell rang, he turned to her.

"Um—this is sort of a weird question, but before this, were you a rental?"

Ashbot froze, reconfigured her face—one of those uncanny moments where she looked genuinely taken by surprise, not like her machinery was processing and forming an adequate response.

"Yeah," she replied flippantly. "But your dad wiped me. I don't remember shit."

(Ever since she and Gideon had the language discussion, she'd been picking it up quite well and sounded nearly normal.)

Naturally, he thought, all that stuff his dad said about making a custom one just for him was bullshit. He should've known.

"Oh. So you don't remember who, um . . . your . . ."

Ashbot shrugged and shook her head. "Nope."

Gideon felt awful—he didn't want her to think he was one of those guys who judged rentals. Those guys were the worst. They'd check out the available Ordinarias and then request their full history just to make sure they weren't getting into any weird territory. Anything unusual on that list, good or bad— NBA players, *Forbes*-list CEOs, famous gay actors who need low-maintenance beards—would make or break whether they rented her.

Jeez . . . since when did he actually *care* about them so much?

"Why do you ask, anyways?" Ashbot cocked her head.

"No reason," he mumbled and silently recited the e-mail over and over and over again. Who had sent it? What did they know? And were they coming for him?

Ashbot lowered her head as they walked, her vivid red hair falling slightly in front of her face. Gideon had a weird urge to brush it away but thought, *Nope, nope, nope.*

"I'll figure it out," she said, still chipper but sounding more melancholy than the regular, empty models he'd grown up with. Sort of like, just because she wasn't programmed to use a melancholy tone, that didn't mean she didn't feel melancholy. But he reminded himself that even though she *seems* like a she, even the most technologically advanced "she" is still an "it." He recited, in his head, his dad's old pitch: *She's not . . . real.*

* * *

There was a rapidly growing club at Pembrooke: the Anti-

Ordinaria Society. They would organize! They would make change! They would force administrators to listen! Or at least they would once they got their shit together.

The problem was that they were from the exact opposite camps. Half of them were girls who didn't shave their armpits and wrote term papers with titles like "Every Sentence Is a Rape." The other half were girls—and a few boys—who wore monogrammed cable-knit sweaters and were insanely jealous of the robots. Mostly they just stayed after school in an empty classroom, ordered pizza (guess which faction of them blotted it), and argued.

That all changed when Anonymous began to mass e-mail them.

Nobody saw her or knew who she was (they assumed it was a her), but since everybody wanted to be in on the secret, everyone insisted they did. Delilah Johnson said she was a faculty member but had sworn not to say whom. Hailey Kissel said it was a friend of hers from another Miss Ordinaria–infested prep school. This is how Anonymous remained that way. If they weren't all so busy tangling their gossip together, they could have tracked her down easily through her e-mails. That was the only way she ever contacted them.

Anonymous sent out e-mail blasts.

You may think you have nothing in common, but you do.

You have the best intentions, pure hearts, and senses of social justice.

If this goes on, it could escalate.

It could kill the entire human race!

We all know how stupid guys are.

They can't be trusted to make good decisions themselves.

That's how every war happened!

Even the Trojan War, which they tried to pin on Helen of Troy. What dicks.

Assemble in the common room at approximately seven P.M. tomorrow.

That is when varsity football practice lets out.

Let's yell at them.

Bye.

These e-mails were massively effective. Very soon, Sumner Ruiz, who had a shaved head and pins through her ears, was walking through the halls chatting excitedly with preppy Betsey Halsey, an old-money heiress to her family's stretch-pants fortune. It was sort of lovely. But it proved abrasive to everyone who wasn't on their growing team.

* * *

Gideon knew it was just a matter of time before they got him. In fact, he wasn't sure why they hadn't already, considering he was the son of the CEO and appearing to openly squire a Miss Ordinaria around school. He was like JFK in the convertible.

But he wasn't concerned with angry mobs. The only thing on his mind was that e-mail. He just couldn't figure it out. He'd scoured the Internet. He'd gone over to Ordinaria Inc. and poked around through some files until a seventy-year-old executive secretary caught him. He had even asked his dad, over a rare "family dinner" at their enormous dining table.

"So . . . is there anyone who, like . . ." Gideon asked tentatively as he watched their maid carve up the too-large roast chicken. "Would want me to know something about myself that I don't know?"

His dad glanced up as he took a sip of his Scotch.

"Not that I know of. Helen?"

He looked at Gideon's mom. She shook her head. She barely spoke.

Then his dad turned back to him, a mean-or-jovial glint in his eye. "You're not coming out, are you?"

Gideon elected not to answer. Instead, he said, "I got a weird e-mail."

"What, like a 'You are part of an unstoppable woman-hating behemoth that will destroy society'? Or one of those ones where some nut job writes to tell you he can fly?"

"Well, neither. It said—"

"Let's not discuss it at the dinner table," his mom said abruptly.

"I agree," his dad said through a mouthful of chicken. "You're a Maclaine. It's part of the territory."

* * *

Every time Ashbot was in the mall, she became a little girl skipping through the daisies. She'd point out the same stores every time as if they were brand-new modern marvels.

"Look, a Talbots!"

Gideon rolled his eyes.

"Ashbot, that was there two days ago. And last week."

She beamed. "I know; it's just so exciting!"

"Why? Why is it so exciting?"

"It's like being with my friends!"

This was so incredibly depressing to Gideon that he went straight to Wendy's to get her a Frosty.

His least favorite part of their regular mall excursion was coming up. It was the giant Victoria's Secret looming across the clear walkway. He had to be the only eighteen-year-old guy who dreaded walking past Victoria's Secret because a girl who liked him wanted to get lacy things.

"We can't stop in there," he said firmly.

"But you're supposed to want me to buy very padded cups!"

Gideon stopped and frowned. He might be losing his mind, but it sounded like something loud and aggressive was going on in there. It was hard to tell, since the whole store was basically one very padded cup.

He snapped away from the distraction. "That—I don't even know wha—look, that doesn't even *sound* appealing."

"Oh. Sorry. Is this better?" She lowered her voice to a sultry whisper. "I want to get some panties for you." Then she stopped and looked confused. "Well, not *for* you—"

"Okay, that's enough."

But Ashbot was already walking inside, a woman-robot on a mission.

I thought you're supposed to listen to me, he thought, irritated, as he followed her.

They walked straight into a fury of shouting, indignant hair tossing, and handmade signs: MISS ORDINARIA IS MIS-GUIDED and GET SEX ROBOTS OUT OF PEMBROOKE. He recognized most of the girls from school. And they recognized him. They immediately started shrieking wordlessly at him, like he was an evil Beatle.

The black-clad Victoria's Secret employees were even more frantic than usual, trying their best to get it under control.

Before Gideon could stop her, Ashbot bypassed her usual favorite, boy shorts with pink on the ass (they were Gideon's favorite too—he had no idea how she'd picked *that* up), and pushed straight into the yelling crowd, as polite and chipper as ever.

"Pardon!"

"Your dad is ruining our school!" shouted a dark-haired girl he recognized from AP Chem.

"Your dad is ruining our *lives!*" sobbed a large girl in a cardigan.

"Jessicarose, weeping isn't constructive," the dark-haired girl snapped.

Their squabble let him slip through the crowd and catch up with Ashbot.

He found her staring up at a giant display of new merchandise, mostly black, red, and white lacy underthings. But this particular line came in only two sizes—two perfect

SCARLETT EPSTEIN HATES IT HERE

sizes based on surveys, research, and years of work. One for a woman aged thirty to fifty, the other for a teenage girl.

The large sign above the underwear table read:

FOR THE *NATURAL* ORDINARIA

(AND NEW MISS ORDINARIA!)

Ashbot looked dazed, like she was having a major revelation. Like whoever first invented fire. Gideon grabbed her arm.

"Come on. Now. We have to get out of here."

The crowd started jeering and snapping thongs at them. A bejeweled one nearly hit Ashbot in the face. Gideon whacked it off course.

As he tried to firmly steer her out, she kept saying, "I get it now! I get it!"

Gideon gritted his teeth, trying not to elbow that sobbing girl in the face as he hustled them both out. "You get what?"

"People are mad because they want to *be* like me."

Her tone was hard for Gideon to read.

Behind him, the protesters engaged in a collective groan/eye-roll situation. And one of them piped up from the way back: "Um, *really*? Anonymous would disagree."

A bolt of lightning struck Gideon.

"Wait—*what* did you just say?"

chapter nine

xLoupxGaroux: FINALLY, a slash couple: Jason/Gideon. Thanks for throwing me a bone.

WillianShipper2000: idk he seems pretty straight to me! :DD

xLoupxGaroux: babe, the ones who try too hard? they always try too hard for a reason.

DavidaTheDeadly: gideon and ashbot! #yasssss #gidbot?

MorwennaWraith: Hey, been lurking on here since the last chapter!! And OMG YES TOTALLY I THOUGHT I'D BE ALONE. #gidbot

WillianShipper2000: they're sooo perfect and Gideon doesn't even know it.

MorwennaWraith: I mean of course he wouldn't want to be with her bc she's his father's invention but . . . romeo and juliet, namsaying?!

DavidaTheDeadly: yes yes yes exactly

MorwennaWraith: #gidbot!! i'm gonna go draw them right now in fact.

DavidaTheDeadly: oh! link when it's up pls. i need a new pic for my cube.

xLoupxGaroux: Anonymous had better be a hot guy, is all I'm saying.

DavidaTheDeadly: this could be such a great character arc for both of them: gideon helps ashbot realize her worth, ashbot helps gideon not take everything so effing seriously . . .

I'm getting nauseated, so I jump in at this point.

Scarface: Guys, she's a robot.

MorwennaWraith: That's not what John would do. He'd make her better than the sum of her parts, LITERALLY

Scarface: But, like . . . maybe she's just a robot. You know?

DavidaTheDeadly: um . . . no? what do you mean? if that's true, who's gideon's otp?

xLoupxGaroux: Then where's the story going? She'll just start and end the same way? That's kind of dull.

Scarface: She's literally one step up from a love doll. She's not his OTP! JESUS. Check yourselves, guys.

xLoupxGaroux: Um, is your DivaCup stuck in you or something? Why are you so worked up about this?

DavidaTheDeadly: when has John ever given us a character that was totally expected? literally 0.00 times; that's what makes him so good.

MorwennaWraith: *Made* him so good. Ugh ugh ughhhh I hate thinking about it.

DavidaTheDeadly: he's not dead.

Scarface: tbh you guys are kinda pissing me off.

xLoupxGaroux Gchats me privately.

xLoupxGaroux: OK. I need to know WTF is making you so upset about this. And don't tell me you're not.

Scarface: Uh . . . idk.

xLoupxGaroux: Seriously, I've never seen you snap at anyone before, even that time people commented on one of your Grecca fics that you stole the concept from *Supernatural*.

Scarface: FOR THE SEVEN MILLIONTH TIME, SIRENS

ARE UBIQUITOUS GREEK MYTHOLOGY THEY'RE NOT ONE PERSON'S "CONCEPT"

xLoupxGaroux: You need a rabies shot.

Scarface: Ugh. Haha. God. I, whatever, I guess I'm weirdly invested because—they're kind of, a tiny bit, based on people I know? Not entirely. I mean, there are no robots in my life, that I know of, so it's obviously not the total truth, I'd say uh—it's the truth *massaged* quite thoroughly.

xLoupxGaroux: You're kidding.

Scarface: TBH I really wanted to keep us together! And writing! And this just seemed easier, as a starting point.

xLoupxGaroux: So, Gideon's a real person??

Scarface: Uh

xLoupxGaroux: YES AND YOU'RE OBSESSED WITH HIM

Scarface: Maybe.

xLoupxGaroux: Do you really go to a private school?

Scarface: HAHA. I wish. I go to a public piece-of-shit school. Inside it's all gray or burnt umber, like a jail. Has anybody in the history of education intellectually flourished inside a "burnt umber" building? I feel like, no. There's always some big asbestos calamity that seems to travel around the building so we're constantly

relocating classes—it's the worst.

xLoupxGaroux: Sounds atrocious. Where do you live?

Scarface: New Jersey.

xLoupxGaroux: That explains it.

Scarface: I know, right? What about you??

xLoupxGaroux: I'm in NYC.

Scarface: NOOOOO

xLoupxGaroux: Yeah!

Scarface: Cannot believe this! I go there all the time! You should give me your cell number, we should hang out next time I'm there! Right??

(xLoupxGaroux is typing . . .)

xLoupxGaroux: yeah def!!

Scarface: I think I'll be around sometime this month (and hopefully after I graduate, for the rest of my life), what times are you usually free??

(xLoupxGaroux is typing . . .)

I hear the front door open, then slam shut, then hushed giggles: Dawn is home with someone. She's whispering, tipsy, but the apartment's small enough for me to catch some of it. "[Something something] not wake her up [something]." More giggles. It's, like, ten. She thinks I go to bed at nine thirty because by then

I'm in my room with the door shut, with no idea I'm on the forum until one or two A.M. every night. Not that she'd care, since I'm not a balding Sears manager who'll pay for her Sea Breeze and mozzarella sticks at Arby's.

As I hear them awkwardly shuffle into Dawn's bedroom, my phone vibrates. It's Ave.

> bad news for you 😭
> gideon just asked ashley to the 💃
> pls don't 😑 🔫

I try to remember that this kind of stuff doesn't really matter. I will not ruin everybody's lunch period tomorrow by repeatedly questioning the fairness of the universe. I will be mature and understanding, gracious and Zen.

I check my Gchat tab. There's still no answer from xLoupxGaroux.

, I text to Ave.

chapter ten

I GRAB MY BOOKS and hustle to social studies, where Mr. Kercher has already started droning hypnotically about Napoléon. I slide into my seat behind Mouth-Breather Leslie, hoping I remain invisible. Jason, Dylan, and—ugh—Gideon have taken to being a little more vocal in class lately. Over the last few weeks, Gideon has grown less startled and quizzical about why the Populars suddenly pulled him into the fold. When I watch him walk with Ashley down the hall, or make some messy ketchup-mayo-mustard concoction out of boredom at lunch with Jason and co., he's undeniably happy. He's one of them now.

". . . few days after he married Josephine, he did . . . what?"

Dead silence.

"He . . . left . . . Paris . . . to . . . ?"

Still nothing. Mr. Kercher is one of the few teachers who

still bothers with this spaced-out-words "hinting" business in the hopes that someone read the textbook chapter assigned for the day. It is excruciating.

"Take . . . command . . . of . . ."

Imagine what would happen if he had a home intruder. ("Hi . . . 911? There's a . . . man . . . in . . . my . . .")

He was young once, which is weird. Maybe he wanted to be an astronaut.

"The . . . army . . . of . . ."

Nothing. Finally, he concedes, sounding dead as he ends with: "Italy, guys. The army of Italy."

He looks around, clearly begging for just one person to be like, *Damn, Italy! It was right on the tip of my tongue.* We respond by staring at him with the glassy eyes of the truly, perhaps even fatally, bored.

"So then, in 1808, he declared that the king of Spain would be his brother, Joseph Bonaparte—"

Snickering from the first-tier popular boys in the back.

"Boner-aparte," says Gideon, putting his comedic stylings to sophisticated use.

They openly crack up. As he laughs and leans back in his chair, Jason tosses his pencil down on the desk for emphasis and further disruption.

"Guys. Please. Please. I'm begging you," beseeches Mr. Kercher.

The back of Mouth-Breather Leslie's head lowers a little, guiltily. She's a Girl Genius, so she knows the answer—but it's easier not to speak up. She's one of those girls whose hair always seems to be hanging in her face in a half-literal, half-metaphorical sort of way. Even if she shaved her head it would still be like that. She does take pity on him, though, and raises her hand tentatively.

"Leslie. Yes."

"Does the Napoleonic Code still affect certain regions of Europe?" she whispers. "I think I read that somewhere."

Mr. Kercher looks at her gratefully.

"Excellent. Yes, Leslie. Some jurisdictions of Europe as well as Africa and . . ."

As he goes on, my pen begins to rattle as I feel Dylan Dinerstein start methodically kicking my chair. (We all sit in those awful Frankenstein-y metal desk/chair mash-ups from the eighties, so everything's connected.) Eventually my pen rolls across the desk and falls.

Instead of telling him to cut it out, I choose the path of least resistance and yank my whole desk and chair farther away from Dylan. It makes a loud, rude noise.

"Yo, Scarlett, did you just fart?" yells Jason.

The other guys snicker, and there are some giggles around the room. Immediately my heart starts pounding like a *Biggest Loser* contestant's, but it's better to ignore him than to dignify it with a response.

I turn around very slightly to look at Gideon, who is not laughing but stubbornly refuses to meet my eye. But then Gideon looks up, smirking, back in the game.

"Nah, I think it was Leslie, man," he says.

Everybody laughs. Leslie slumps even lower, her head down.

Mr. Kercher holds up his hands. "Guys. Guys." Nobody listens.

It's one thing to pick on me, but Leslie can't stand up for herself.

I wheel around and snap, "Nope! Totally me. Really important investigation, Jason. Thanks for spreading awareness."

"Everybody just calm down," says Mr. Kercher.

Jason just gives me a *Crazy bitch* stare, infuriatingly blank and slack-jawed.

"Nothing?" My eyes dart over to Gideon, who still refuses to look at me. I get louder.

"You have nothing to say?"

Mr. Kercher finally loses it, banging his palm down on his desk.

"Scarlett, that's enough!"

He sends me to the front office, where I get a pink detention slip to forge Dawn's signature on.

As Ave, the Girl Geniuses, and I walk past the Populars to get our lunch trays, Ashley studiously pays no attention to Ave. You'd think they were strangers, not sisters, but there is no sibling loophole for breaking the MHS caste system.

Gideon heads for a table at the nuclear center of a group of loud jock guys, chatting with Mike Tossier in the dulcet tones of loud bro. He glances at me, and I give him my best glare. He looks away. I wonder, again, what the hell is going on—why Ashley would pick Gideon, loaning her much-curated social life to him. Either he struck some kind of Faustian bargain or Ashley is actively trying to ruin my life.

We sit down at the designated Girl Genius table with the other lady misanthropes. A few fey, antisocial boys who look twelve sit here too, for good measure.

"Yes, this is my cheap-ass poor-person lunch," I announce when I sit down with my tray, and they laugh, like they do every time. I used to try to hide swiping my reduced-lunch card, but eventually I realized I can neutralize it with jokes, make people feel more comfortable and less like I'm some walking PSA.

"Hey, Ave?" I ask.

"Yeah?" She pulls out a bag full of almonds and pops one in her mouth.

"Have I told you lately . . . that I love you?"

Avery rolls her eyes, crunching. "What do you want?"

"Can you do my take-home test? It's due next period." I yank it from my folder and hand it to her. She pulls out a ballpoint— the true sign of a math genius, not picking a pencil—and starts efficiently scribbling in answers, moving from equation to equation without missing a beat.

"One of these days I'm gonna tell my parents about this," she threatens, then rolls her eyes. "Actually, it wouldn't matter. You could murder a drifter and they'd still love you."

She might act cranky, but she likes doing it. She told me once that it's relaxing to do my tests because they're so easy that it's like a form of supersmart-person meditation. Not that she said it in those words, she's always been way too modest. (If Ave had invented fire, she'd introduce it to the Cro-Magnons by whispering, "Um, hey, I made this thing, it's kinda cool, it might be sorta helpful for our continued evolution, if that makes any sense.")

As Ave whizzes through my test, occasionally sipping one of the many cans of Diet Coke she guzzles all day, there's a shuffling behind us, then a shadow over poor Got Her Period on Her Pants and Nobody Told Her Leslie like one cast by the side of a mountain.

It's Mike Neckekis, a tree-trunk-neck jock who in the days of yore might have been called "simple." Ave doesn't notice.

I nudge her. "Um . . . Avery?"

She glances up and around. Looks at Mike. Waits expectantly. Generally speaking, the Populars approach Avery only if they want to buy Adderall, pay her to write their college essay, or ask if she and Ashley are *really* sisters.

"I wanted to say that uh, uh . . ." He breathes heavily, in what would seem like a sigh if it was not just his natural state of Pop-Tarts-infused mouth breathing. "Uh . . ."

We all stare.

"I agreed with you in sociology when Mrs. Donovan was talking about Twitter outrage, and you argued that was a privileged point of view."

"I didn't . . . did I argue that?"

"Well, you sort of mumbled it. You mumble stuff."

"I do?"

"Yeah, you mumble stuff, and you scratch your forehead with your pen, and sometimes the cap is off, so you get, um . . ." He runs his finger over his hairline. "Ink stains. Not right now, but sometimes."

Avery stares at him for a second, touching her forehead self-consciously. She looks perplexed, but sort of . . . happy? How can she not be laughing her ass off at him right now?

"Anyways, I agree with you. I think, like, Twitter totally scares snobs like Mrs. Donovan who live in, like, mansions in Short Hills and commute here to teach because they want to feel like they're helping out less rich people without actually having to, like, think about them all that much. So. Yeah."

Avery breaks into a smile.

"I was wondering—I saw you talking to some older guy when you were getting off the Princeton bus, and I wasn't sure if you were, like, dating . . ."

"We're not," Ave says, still smiling, seeming shell-shocked. "I mean. No. Nothing is—he's not my boyfriend. Or anything. I was asking him if we'll still have a free period."

"Oh! Okay. Well. I guess, then, do you want to go to the dance with me?"

Avery's jaw drops in the briefest expression of pure joy before she tamps it down, undoubtedly due to the numerous dating-advice listicles Dawn posts on our Facebook walls with headlines like "17 Ways to Win at Love by Pretending You Don't Give a Crap."

"I wasn't gonna go, but . . . if you think that would be fun, then sure, why not," she says casually. Seriously, does everybody know how to fake unenthusiasm but me?

Mike actually does sigh this time, I think, of relief. "Cool. Okay. I got your number from Ashley."

Our entire table simultaneously looks over at Ashley, who's already been glaring at us with comical menace, like an owl antagonist in a children's movie about mice.

"So, I'll text you my number, and, like, then we can have each other's . . . numbers? So we can text?"

Avery nods, smiles. "Sounds good."

As soon as he walks away, I nearly blow a gasket finally letting my derision fly. "Mike fucking Neckekis?!"

"Chill out." Avery lets out a breathless laugh and drops her head in her hands. I watch her shoulders shaking with laughter. But it's not the derisive kind I expected. It's more like "just got off a roller coaster" exhilaration.

I'm wounded. She's been holding out on me.

"And you never told me abou—who's the guy in your math class at Princeton?" Everybody else at our table is poker-faced because they are all basically feral brains without bodies.

"We're auditing," Ave says, pulling a lip balm out of her book bag's front pocket and pouting to nonchalantly apply it. Two boys say hi to her, and suddenly she's Lana Del Rey. "Technically none of us are in our math class at Princeton."

"Come on, you know what I mean."

"Yes, he tested out of the math classes. Same as me."

"Well, that makes a little more sense, doesn't it?"

Ave looks pointedly at me. "What do you mean?"

"What do you mean, what do I mean? That means he's smart, and probably more right for you than Mike Neckekis, who is Comic Sans in human form."

She shrugs. "We obviously agree on some stuff."

"Oh, so someone jerks you off intellectually, and now you're into him? What are you, a *guy* now?"

The Girl Geniuses' eyes dart back and forth between us, the two alphas of the table, like they're watching a tennis match.

Ave slowly rolls her head toward me with wide, infuriated eyes, a sassy Linda Blair *Exorcist* move she does when I've really pissed her off.

"He's nice, Scar."

I almost scream. *Nice?* Nice is staying in Melville and planning a low-budget indoor wedding at the Freehold Gardens Mall Event Center to some guy from high school who works at Target. None of which I say out loud because her head would spin a complete 360 degrees, and I don't want to lose the only real friend I have in my age bracket.

"You're right," I say. "I'm sorry. I'm being a dick."

Avery softens a little, then, looking at my contrite face, melts the rest of the way. "It's okay." Then she smiles again, a smile I rarely see. "I have no idea what to wear. What do girls wear to this stuff?"

"Ask Ashley if she has any Taylor Swift crop-top formal-gown castoffs you can borrow," I joke. (This is the precise ludicrous taffeta bullshit Ashley wore to junior prom.) And just like that, we're friends again. That's how we fight—intense and mean, and then it's over in the blink of an eye. Maybe that's how sisters are.

But one tectonic plate of our friendship has destructively scraped up against another. Like Ave's finally been taken by the other team of Red Rover, and now I'm facing off against the whole senior class, their normal, optimistic, sexually active arms linked tight.

Sometimes my entire high school experience feels like being the only one who already knows the end of a movie, when everyone else you're going with is so excited to see how the movie will end. Spoiler alert: a 20 percent discount at Target.

chapter eleven

AS SOON AS I'M HOME from school, barely in the door, I throw my laptop on the nearest possible flat surface (this time, the side table) and check the Lycanthrope tabs. Days after I posted the second story, the number of readers—and Gidbot shippers—is growing.

I can't decide if I'm flattered or deeply irritated.

I scroll through the gushing and hashtags and cries of "YAAAAAS" and roll my eyes.

The problem is that if I smash Ashbot with a crowbar, everyone will yell at me and only ship the couple *more*. And . . . to be honest, I'll be sad too. I like her; she came out differently than I expected. I never knew original(-ish) characters could be sneaky like that.

I guess the only thing I can do is create a diversion. . . .

The Ordinaria
Part 3

Submitted by Scarface_Epstein

Creating Miss Ordinaria was a little bit like creating a women's magazine. A ton of work was done, undone, and done again, and everything was based on endless studies and surveys and data, but somehow it always ends up as the lowest common denominator. Something that looks like no work was put into it at all.

But before the prototype went through the wringer and came out as the robot-girl equivalent of a beach read, one of the many studies involved handpicking a few teenage girls who embodied certain qualities that had rated well. The physical stuff was easy—testable. But building an appealing personality from scratch is way more subjective. So when they picked the girls, looks weren't an issue. Maybe they didn't have the glossy hair, the perfect figure, or the indiscriminating sexual freedom, but they had other skills: violin playing, perfect pitch, 4.0 GPA, years of grooming for the nationals in figure skating, and so on.

The plan was to narrow down the top four categories that teenage boys looked for in a girl's personality, search across the country for girls that best represented each category, and then contain them in the lab for five months in order to thoroughly observe their behavior.

Ava was an obvious candidate for one of the slots:

intelligence. She entered only because her mother was determined she continue her studies at a top university, and being chosen would diversify her application, supplementing her excellent grades. She quickly made it past the preliminary interviews, then the finals, and made it through. (There was no broadcast on TV; networks uniformly turned it down, saying that even if there was a swimsuit element—which there wasn't—nobody would tune in to see *normal* girls wearing them.)

The other slots, determined by a nationwide survey of men in an extremely wide demographic, were philanthropy, creativity, and educational voraciousness. The girls chosen were from all over the country: Tara, seventeen, had started volunteering at homeless shelters at age thirteen and was now a Goodwill Ambassador for the UN. Jill, eighteen, was an art prodigy whose abstract paintings had been shown at MoMA and the Sorbonne. Jen, sixteen, was a pretty normal girl who didn't know anything about cool stuff but really, really wanted to be introduced to it, which showed a deep interest in art, music, film, programming, culture, and education at large. (When surveyed, the feedback from consumers was that Ordinarias would sit patiently as the men talked at length about noise bands, HTML, or Hemingway but never seemed to listen or appreciate the invaluable cultural education the men were so thoughtfully attempting to give the Ordinarias.)

Ava couldn't have cared less about any of this, but to appease her mom, she spent the required five-month quarantine at the rebuilt headquarters, taking standardized subject tests and personality quizzes from Ordinaria engineers. The four girls shared two bunk beds above the lab, and the only thing they seemed to have in common was ulterior motives for being there, which they occasionally discussed late at night, in the dark.

"Well, *I'm* here only because I want to improve conditions at the factory. Did you know they're paid only slightly above minimum wage?" said Tara, who was either heartfelt or sanctimonious depending on one's mood.

"I'm here because I'm researching a multimedia installation that breaks down modern American femininity," said Jill, who wore all black and read Sylvia Plath when she wasn't in the lab, painting an abstract with electrodes taped to her forehead and engineers taking notes.

Jen cleared her throat. "Do you guys know anything about the Smiths?"

"No," they all said. (Jill was lying, but she'd already had to talk to Jen about the Kinks, the Clash, and the Shins; she was done.)

"Me neither," Jen said plaintively.

* * *

It was raining outside, for the third day straight, but Ava would still do anything for some fresh air. They weren't allowed to leave—since they were test subjects, the engineers were paranoid that other people would try to influence them.

Ava crept out of the holding pen and tiptoed down the

hall. Breaking rules made her nervous, and she was deciding whether to turn back or go ahead and push through the contraband side-exit door—just for a breath of air—when it swung open and a dripping-wet guy lumbered in. He saw her, and they both stood there for a second, realizing that both of them would get in trouble if the other one told.

"Are you one of those girls?" he asked. That's what they called them. They didn't really have a name for this five-month stretch.

She nodded.

"What are you doing out here?"

"I was just gonna . . . who are *you*?" she asked defensively.

"Oh. Um, name's Mike. I'm just a deliveryman. I was on the highway with my truck"—he motioned to an enormous truck with Ordinaria Inc. painted over the company's trademark logo, a curvy female silhouette—"but the rain got too bad, so I figured I'd pull in and wait it out. I've been driving for nine hours or so; my eyes were getting tired."

He was around her age. He spoke slowly, she noticed, and fumbled words a lot. She found it endearing and couldn't help but notice how his wet clothes had conformed to the outline of his very nice body. At that moment, they thought they heard the echoes of footsteps.

"Why don't we move to the loading dock?" he asked. She hesitated, then nodded.

* * *

Over the next few weeks, secretly, they got to know each other better. Mike was from a few towns over from Ava's. He hadn't gotten into the academy, so when he'd turned seventeen, he became an Ordinaria deliveryman, like his father and grandfather had. He was a little bit in awe of her, and she was surprised how much she liked it, considering she hated the attention she'd always gotten from her mother, teachers, and fellow students for her intelligence. She'd always thought she'd feel this attracted only to another star student.

It became a weekly ritual: They'd meet on the loading dock, swinging their legs over the edge. He'd give her a piece of regional candy he'd gotten from whatever state he had to drive from, and they'd talk about their day, or the candy, or the weather, or whatever. They didn't have a lot in common, and there were a lot of long silences, but they were packed with enough crackling sexual tension to fill entire books.

One afternoon, after his long drive back from New England, he gave her a maple sugar leaf. On this day, there was an unusual sense of urgency. Ava was coming to the end of her quarantine, and she was afraid they'd never see each other again. Rather than sitting, they stood, facing each other, him towering over her.

She unwrapped the leaf and started self-consciously blushing as she sucked on it while he watched.

"Want some?" She held it out to him. Instead, he pushed her back against the brick wall of the loading dock and kissed her. All other thoughts floated out of her head, including what—or who—she might be leaving behind.

chapter twelve

DAWN EMERGES FROM THE BATHROOM and glides toward me like an incredibly round and bizarre debutante and twirls in her white boots, pulled up over flimsy fishnets. The prospect of a "slutty green M&M" seems impossible, but there can be miracles when you believe.

"So? How do I look?"

"Like anthropomorphic candy."

She rolls her eyes. "I mean, obviously. But I mean my hair and makeup."

"Good."

Her face flashes that this is the wrong answer, considering she has just spent two hours in the bathroom getting ready.

"No, *great*!" I say more enthusiastically. "But why don't you just go out on Halloween proper instead?" I sigh. "I'm worried you're gonna get Clockwork Oranged."

It's October 30——Mischief Night. It is exactly what it sounds like: an excuse for MHS students to truly be the creepy, ultraviolent droogs they are. They smash pumpkins on doorsteps, toilet paper people's houses and cars, and generally act like the stupid, reckless kids the cops always think did it in the first fifteen minutes of *Law & Order*.

"Scar, it'll be fine. I won't be out and about or anything. Brian invited me to his office party!" She beamed. "It's one of those haunted houses where there's punch, and you get blindfolded and put your hand in a thing of peeled grapes."

"Sounds gripping. Use protection."

Dawn sighs and puts her hands on her (actual) waist, folding her costume from totally circular into a cinched figure eight.

"I realize that it'll be an awful ordeal for you, sweetie, but you *will* have to meet him at some point."

"Really? 'Cause I'm totally comfortable with keeping him a concept."

"Well, he really wants to meet you-uuuuu," she says, practically singing the last word.

This is mildly disconcerting because usually they don't want to meet me. Usually, since she knows I'm a harsher judge of character, she wants me to meet——and evaluate——them. In fact, on one notable occasion, Dawn pretended I did not even exist (which culminated in the Great "I'm Not a Good Mother" Crying Jag of 2012). So I'm briefly at a loss for words.

"Well, I don't know." I shrug. "Tell him to bring me an expensive bottle of wine and a sacrificial virgin."

Then she zings me: "You *are* a sacrificial virgin."

I suck in my breath. "Daaaaaaayum, I ought to call CP&P for that one."

(Child Protection & Permanency plucks New Jersey kids out of "inadequate households" and places them in the state's care. It is also Dawn's and my best inside joke, because we're sick people.)

As she heads for the door, she pulls some money out of God knows where and leaves it a few feet away on the kitchen island.

"Order a pizza or something, okay?"

"Yep."

I glance down and notice that her legs are practically bare, covered only by the sheer tights.

"Yo, aren't you gonna wear something over that?" I call after her. "It's kinda cold out."

She and the pair of eyes on the green M&M costume both stare haughtily at me. "Chocolate can't wear jackets," she says matter-of-factly, as if I am supposed to smack my forehead like, *Oh, right, how could I forget that famous old adage, "Chocolate can't wear jackets"*?

"Have fun! Be safe! Say hi to Brian!" I yell after her as she opens the door with a loud gust of wind and slams it abruptly behind her.

I'm not a total shithead. I've met a few of her boyfriends, mostly at awkward third-wheel dinners at this one Mediterranean place downtown that we use only for her boyfriends. If she marries one of them, it'll be kind of fun to yell "YOU'RE NOT

MY REAL DAD!" at him and storm away to my room, although a two-floor house would really make for better storming. Storming in an affordable-housing apartment means you go two loud, impotent stomps away and you're, like, already in your room. It's not worth the effort.

I glance outside and watch as she runs to the Taurus, shivering, just to make sure no assholes pop out of the bushes with water guns or eggs.

Being primarily friendless, and also somewhat intelligent, I'm staying in. Halloween stuff doesn't scare me easily, but when this many teenagers in town are congregated in permissive parents' basements doing shots of 151 and preparing to smash in some car windows, you can sort of feel the weird destructive electricity in the air.

I feast on a balanced meal of pizza and a coffee mug filled with some white wine Dawn left uncorked on the side of the fridge, squeezed in between the eggs and milk. Then I read a little bit of Kira's novel, *Genius Family*, right up to the part where her brilliant and beautiful but aloof physics-prodigy mother makes subtle fun of the soccer moms at the PTA but they're too stupid to notice. I Google Kira again and read some new reviews, one of which is in the *Washington Post*: "A solid debut," albeit "just a touch self-consciously quirky and smug." Ouch. I wonder how she'd respond to that. She's probably above it all. I think it's easy for beautiful people to be above things.

By around ten I'm lying in bed and lulling myself to sleep chatting with Were-Heads about random stuff, because that's the thrilling life I lead.

I'm half-asleep when I turn my head toward the window and see some movement across the highway, in front of Ruth's place. I sit up and pull my curtain aside to see four small, dark figures standing—posturing, really—one of them holding a nearly empty squarish bottle by its long neck, glinting in the porch light. Their steps, somehow, are barely making any noise.

Simultaneously two rolls of toilet paper soar in an arc against the dark sky toward Ruth's roof, and then comes the splat of an egg. I realize they're in the garden, their Sperrys mashing and ruining Ruth's flowers. That's why their sneakers are padding silently on the ground. Ruth is almost certainly sound asleep by now; she has been going to bed earlier and earlier. If this wakes her up, she's sure to be wrecked tomorrow.

Suddenly I'm so angry I can hardly feel my body, other than my face getting so hot it feels like my head might explode. My body, meanwhile, is jumping out of bed, yanking on Dawn's Uggs by the front door and leaving it wide open behind me as I fly down the stairs and march toward them with a flashlight. I barely check for cars before I'm tearing across the highway.

"Hey!"

Jason Tous stands there casually, like he's waiting for a bus, but the other three—who I can't make out—take off, winding around Ruth's house and running into the pitch-black woods that crawl almost all the way up to her side door. I take off after them.

We are all quickly swallowed up by the darkness and the quiet, every branch snapping under our shoes sounding like gunshots.

"Yo!" I shout.

One of the guys drops an empty bottle in his haste, and I snag it, barely slowing down. Jack Daniels—of course, patron saint of boys who try too hard to be Men. I hurl the bottle at the slowest boy as hard as I can, and it glances off his shoulder blade with the *whack* of glass on bone.

"Fuck!" he yelps, stopping to crouch and massage his shoulder. One of the other two keeps running, but one slows to a stop, looking back to see if the injured one is okay. I shine my flashlight in that guy's face and actually *gasp*—as if I am on a soap opera and just caught my estranged evil twin making out with my husband—because it's Gideon. I mean, of course it is. I'm surprised, and not surprised, and that combination takes my voice away for a few seconds, but fortunately I get my words back.

"Seriously?" My voice verges on shrieking. The injured boy— it's Dylan Dinerstein—is still rubbing his shoulder and looking sullen, but I'm addressing Gideon. "What's *wrong* with you?"

He shakes his head minutely, and I think I see a flicker of something in his face—guilt maybe—but he says nothing.

"That's the problem with you assholes," I snap. "You have nothing to say. So you pick on people who do."

I can't look at Gideon anymore—with him it's way too complicated. But the other guys? They're anything but. The words fly off my tongue before they're filtered by my brain.

"Know what? I *hope* you get monster boners when you wreck

an old lady's house, or when you make Leslie Barnes feel like shit for raising her hand. In ten years, Leslie Barnes will be running a million-dollar company—but you'll still be here, still doing this, for the rest of your life. She won't even come back for reunions. And neither will I, bitches."

From behind me, Jason walks into my line of vision, keeping his head down. It seems like I may have struck a chord, but I'm too high on adrenaline to really know. He gestures to the other guys, and they stalk out of the woods in the direction of a stretch of main road where kids always park their cars when they come to drink.

I trudge the opposite way, resisting every temptation to look back at Gideon, and end up at the edge of Ruth's wrecked garden, surveying the damage. A line has been crossed. He's just not the same person anymore, right? He wears their dumb clothes and teases their weak targets. Still, the same little hopeful recorded message plays over and over in my head: *Maybe the short, chubby comedy nerd is still in there somewhere!* At what point do you start writing off the only person who you thought really got you?

I hear the shutter door bounce twice, and before I can warn her, Ruth pops out, wide-eyed, in an uncharacteristically feminine kimono with her hair in a scrunchie high on her head.

"Are you okay?" I ask Ruth.

"I'm fine. I was sleeping." She surveys her garden.

"Do you want me to . . ." I helplessly sort of move my hands around in a way that feels appropriately sympathetic. She shakes her head.

"We can't do anything about it tonight. Besides, it's easy to grow them back."

Still, I'm mad on her behalf. "Ugh, those guys are—"

"Those aren't guys; they're *kids*. Please, go to bed. You can help me take care of it tomorrow if you want. This is way too much late-night excitement for someone past menopause."

She sighs, a brief cloud passing over her usual laissez-faire attitude.

Even if she'd never admit it, I know how much she loves looking at her garden.

Back in bed but wide-awake, I wonder if I even know Gideon, or know anyone really. Is this the moment I'm supposed to realize Gideon's actually a shitty person who just happens to have excellent taste in comedy? Or is this the moment I realize I'm too judgmental and living in my own weird cerebral universe and have unrealistic standards for boys, or just for life?

It's been bothering me more and more that I can't ever see anything objectively, that every observation I make is filtered through my personal lens whether I like it or not. I mean, all my favorite novels are like that. F. Scott Fitzgerald basically *is* Gatsby, so obviously it's Gatsby's book, and Daisy comes off like a flake. But maybe in Daisy's unwritten book, Gatsby is a flashy, patronizing asshole who thinks he could win her with money and fancy stuff. And that might be an even better book.

Eventually, sometime around when dawn breaks and I hear

the jingle of Dawn's keys landing on the kitchen island, I fall asleep wishing more than anything that I could float outside my head and see things for what they truly, honestly, objectively are . . . and kill the tiny voice in my head that constantly questions whether that truth even exists.

Whatever. One thing at a time.

chapter thirteen

THANKS TO THE MORONIC shuffling of Jason Tous—
I can tell by the imprint that it was his neon green-and-yellow
Air Jordans—the zinnias cannot be salvaged. But some of the
American Beauty roses are okay, and the snapped lavender
bunches can be dried and hung. (Ruth is not the sort of person
who would do that, but Dawn is at least the sort of person who
would make an obsessive Pinterest board full of intricately hung
dried lavender and then not do it.)

"I'm gonna come back and fix this as best I can tomorrow,
okay?" I ask.

Ruth shrugs and nods. I can tell she's still pretending she
doesn't care as much as she does about her flowers. Apparently
there is no expiration date on this "pretending not to care"
nonsense. I have a hunch that she thinks openly caring that much
about a garden is encroaching on *Tuesdays with Morrie* territory.

Instead, I focus on the eggs, which oozed like gross gelatinous grenade-lumps on Ruth's roof until they half froze in the chill. As I scrape and wipe them away, the smell of weed drifts tellingly by. Underneath me, Ruth is sitting on her porch, wearing the same rumpled high ponytail she slept in. She's vaping. Who the hell got her a vaporizer?

"I'm gonna pay you extra for this," says Ruth.

"No, don't." I make a face as I shovel the remnants of one cracked egg into the plastic bag on my arm.

"What?" she yells from below.

"Don't pay me extra!" I call back. I think agreeing on a certain amount of money an hour is fair, but I don't like bonuses; they always feel like charity.

"That's very sweet of you," she says.

Finished, I sidle on my butt over to the ladder, climb down a few rungs, and jump the rest of the way. I wipe my flat palms together with a sense of accomplishment.

"Your roof is normal."

"Not as long as I'm living under it," she quips.

"That's true." I peel the disgusting icicle-eggy gloves off and balance them on the porch rail.

"So . . . it's a destruction holiday," Ruth says, trying to grasp the concept of Mischief Night, which I explained to her as I prepared for aborted-chicken-zygote battle this morning.

"In essence."

She exhales a white cloud that lazily rises. "Did you *know* them?"

"Yeah, they go to my school."

She nods, a small reaction, because she probably guessed.

"What did *you* do last night?" she asks with a pointed tone that I don't like.

"Lost my temper. You know what I did last night." I busy myself picking flecks of egg off the gloves and flicking them away.

"You didn't go out?"

I wrinkle my nose. "No."

"What was Avery doing?"

"I have no idea. Probably studying for the SATs." *Probably studying for Mike Neckekis's junk.*

"You didn't want to go out with the boys who came here?" She makes it sound like they came over to sip Arnold Palmers and play charades.

"Uh, no."

"Why not?"

"Because I'm not a douche."

Ruth shrugs, vapes delicately with her pinkie in the air, and lets it go again. "When I was your age . . ."

"You prank called a stegosaurus?"

"Very funny. Actually, whenever we had a bad substitute teacher, I'd get the whole class to throw their textbooks on the floor very hard, and he'd reflexively duck under his desk— that's what we were taught to do during the war if a bomb fell."

"Dark."

"You should take advantage of your youth while you've got it.

Drink some whiskey. Spend some time with boys—or girls, if you want. Egg an old lady's house."

I make a *Come on* face.

"Not for you?" she asks, sounding amused.

"I'm not an asshole."

"You're sixteen. By the time you're twenty-one, they'll expect you to be a real person. This is your asshole window. It's wide open."

"Ew, don't talk about my asshole window."

"I just wish you'd raise a little hell! You know? Soon it'll be too late."

"Um, too late? I think I've got a while."

"You really never know how much time you've got." She looks off into the distance for a second, focusing on something far away. Then she snaps back into the present. "For instance, I read in the newspaper today that a lovely straight-A student at the Hun School passed away last week."

"Oh. That sucks."

"She snorted too much Molly."

"I don't think you snort Molly."

"Well, she snorted too much *something*."

"Who even snorts things anymore? Like, just take it with water. Who are you, Bret Easton Ellis?"

"Scarlett, she *died*," snaps Ruth very uncharacteristically. "Everything is a joke to you." It startles me enough to shut me right up. I scrape egg in silence for a minute. She sighs and rubs her temples with two fingers each, nails painted bright green.

She wears zero makeup but lives for gel manicures—one of the zillion Ruth contradictions I'm obsessed with.

"Sorry. All I'm trying to say is . . . you know. Live in the moment. Get a little nuts. Life is short."

I shrug. "To be honest, it kind of feels like my life hasn't started yet."

"Kiddo," Ruth says, "your life started the minute you put pen to paper."

I roll my eyes. But maybe she's right. She *is* seven thousand years old.

After I've returned home and washed the egg off my person, Dawn and I sit on the sofa and devour a large half-mushroom pie. Every local takeout guy is more or less a member of our extended family at this point. On TV, some *Real Housewives* or another flickers on mute.

"I think next week we should have dinner with Brian," she says mildly, blotting her second slice with her French-manicured hand.

"Which one is that? Bald or Balder?"

She eyeballs me. "Brian. *Brian.* The only guy I've been dating for the last two weeks."

"Yeah, sure, whatever."

She props her arm on the back of the couch, leaning in toward me, a worry line creasing her forehead.

"Are you all right?" she asks.

"Fine," I mumble.

She brightens. "Guy trouble?"

"No! Guys aren't the only thing girls are sad about. Jesus." (I'm mostly irritated that she's right.)

"I was just asking." She sounds hurt, and I feel a twinge of guilt.

My cell phone rings. I beam.

"Dad!" I say, holding up the phone and already hopping off the chair. She nods blankly, the usual reaction, and I walk away from the kitchen table into my room. I shut the door, intentionally fueling her paranoid—and *mostly* inaccurate—suspicion that all I do when I'm on the phone with him is complain about her. I sometimes do, but he never does. Honestly, Dawn worries that he talks tons of shit on her to me only because she talks tons of shit on him to me.

I slide my thumb over the phone to accept the call. "Hi!"

"Hey, Scarlett!" Just hearing his familiar, comforting voice is calming, especially when he says, "How ya holding up?"

I don't even have to ask what he means by that: He knows the *Lycanthrope* cancellation broke my heart. If you want humor and understanding, you go to Dad. If you want to determine if a Louis Vuitton bag you bought on eBay is real or not, you go to Dawn.

"Other than my abject devastation, I'm okay." I sigh.

"I know," he says warmly. "Hang in there."

"I'm trying."

"I just keep thinking how unfair it is that it never won an

Emmy," he says, sounding genuinely incredulous. "Just because it's not some hour-long HBO miniseries. Those pretentious idiots."

"Yeah, that's what a lot of the fandom has been saying. Indignation Central over there."

He laughs quietly. "What other responses have there been?"

I shrug. "Most people are moving on. I think mostly the migration is to that CW show *Imaginary Detectives*."

"And you?"

"I'm sticking around."

"Loyal."

"To a fault." I sigh, fake-dramatically.

"Have you started my present yet?" he asks.

"Oh, you mean that doorstop full of papers?"

Dad sent me some books—*The Corrections* and *Infinite Jest*—for my birthday.

"I haven't gotten around to it," I admit, "but I will really soon, I promise."

I wonder if I should tell Dad about the Gideon situation. We don't usually talk about guy stuff outside the weird metaphorical father/daughter talks based on TV shows and novels we've read, but it's still bothering me a lot, and maybe he has advice.

"So, Dad, I—"

"I've got some news!" Dad cuts me off, then makes a fuzzy noise that I realize is a deep breath.

"Oh. Bad or good?"

"Good." He clears his throat. "Great, actually."

"John St. Clair's wife actually had a hysterical pregnancy, and the show will be back on next season?" I ask hopefully.

"My book launch party is a couple of weeks from now. Friday, the eighteenth."

I shriek with joy.

"Jesus. Scarlett, my ears."

"Oh my God! Are you serious? Dad, that's awesome! God, it's been years!"

"That's the funny thing. I mean, I wrote it years ago, obviously. In fact, when I was still married to your mother. Ha-ha!" He laughs nervously. "Although Kira helped me quite a bit with the last revision."

Of course she did. The vision of Kira and Dad brewing some French press coffee and spending a lazy Saturday morning in the brownstone going over line edits almost makes me hurl with aspirational envy.

"Dad, that's amazing. Seriously. You're gonna be famous. And I am *so* gonna benefit from that sweet, sweet literary-world nepotism."

He laughs. "Let's not get our hopes up just yet. It still feels very surreal."

"Well, get used to it, pretty soon it'll be very real!"

"That's true," he says, sounding way more measured and low-key than I'd expect from a debut novelist who has been working on this manuscript since I was eight.

"Don't sound so elated; you might sprain something."

"What about you?" he asks. Being typically modest, of course he is changing the subject. I reluctantly roll with it.

"What about me?"

"It's about time I saw some of your work, isn't it?"

"It's *fan*fiction, I'm not Alice Munro. And to answer your question, I'll send something to you when you have the hookup at the *New Yorker*."

"Scar, I mean it. I might not have a ton of time right now because of all the book stuff, but I really want to read them. I know you've been at the top of the pack in this community for years. When can I see them?"

"When they're good enough for you to read," I say.

"I have no doubt that they already are."

I brush that off, insisting I'll send one soon, but all the while a warm, loved feeling creeps up behind my rib cage like ivy.

chapter fourteen

The Ordinaria
Part 4
Submitted by Scarface_Epstein

It was the night of the Pembrooke donors' ball, when all the wealthy parents who had swimming pools or lacrosse courts in their names were rewarded with highballs, a live band, and zero mentions of the money. That would be déclassé.

Gideon's father had basically strong-armed him into hanging out with Jason Tous and his two flunkies from school. Now here they were in his foyer, in impeccably tailored suits, sitting on stiff-backed chairs in the laboratory waiting room as Ashbot and the other (human) girls got ready upstairs.

His father, naturally, really liked these obnoxious guys—

not to mention zeroed in on them as potential Miss Ordinaria consumers. Some of them had even applied to intern at the lab.

Gideon hated it at first . . . but then he surprised himself. Getting wasted and making sexual jokes about "product testing" was kind of fun. He would be lying if he said he didn't enjoy hanging with them just a little bit, having a beer with some normal guys and pretending he was one too, at least for a little while.

He noticed he was jiggling his leg nervously and stopped. Usually these things were incredibly boring, and he went only because his parents made him. Not this time. He'd gotten another e-mail from Anonymous last night: **I'll be at the donors' ball. Black dress. We need to talk.**

It was the first he'd heard from Anonymous since the original e-mail. Black dress! So it was a woman (probably). He was determined to get to the bottom of it. He just hoped there weren't too many women in black dresses—he really didn't want to go up to someone cool-looking and ask, "Are you Anonymous?" like a noir blind date.

He sighed, audibly.

Jason was slumped insolently in his chair checking his phone, with his legs spread much wider than they needed to be. He glanced at Gideon, then broke into an Ol' Boy grin and slapped him on the back.

"You've got it made, dude! Lighten up."

"Nah, it's not chill." When he was with them, Gideon slid into colloquialisms he'd never use normally. The other day in

AP Philosophy, he actually heard himself say, "Proust was dope." Everyone laughed, even the teacher. With him, though. Not at him. It gave him a proud rush.

Dylan Dinerstein, usually the quietest, piped up: "I get it. You don't want to settle on one. You want to rent a little first, and now you're stuck with—"

He jerked his head toward the stairs.

"It's not even like that," Gideon mumbled.

"You won't even feel, like . . . obligated to put a down payment on her once she's got a lot of miles on her."

"Miles?"

"Hi!"

Ashbot stood at the top of the stairs, flanked by the other three guys' dates, who were all wearing black. Ashbot had finally found her clique: the sort of girls who dated guys like Jason and blotted their pizza and wore Miss Ordinaria–brand lingerie. Still, of course, Ashbot looked hotter than all of them. She was wearing a white dress that flattered her pale, creamy skin. Then they glided down the marble stairs, their four-inch heels clacking perfectly in time with one another.

Gideon held out his arm and Ashbot took it, smiling brightly at him and tossing her hair, accidentally showing the on-off switch on the back of her neck. He fixed her hair to cover it again.

She zeroed in on his yellow tie. "Oh, you have to change that. Quick, we'll be late."

"What's up with that? They look like they're going to a funeral."

Ashbot rolled her eyes. "God, did you even look at the invite? It's a black-and-white ball."

Gideon groaned. "Goddamn it."

* * *

Since it was also the year of the Miss Ordinaria test run, and press would be there, the celebration this year was bigger than usual. Fancier. A crowd of people clustered outside the gates in cocktail attire, trying to fake their way in by saying some invented relative was a dearly departed donor.

"Laaaame," Peter sighed, barely looking up from his game app.

"Baby, stop," whined his girlfriend, tugging at his tux sleeve.

As their driver handed the limo keys to the valet, Gideon made his way toward the ballroom with Ashbot, wincing from the flashbulbs of press and paparazzi that usually followed a Maclaine at a social event. It didn't faze Ashbot, naturally, and the photos would end up looking great, which was the reason so many actresses were Ordinarias passed off as real by their managers and agents: nary an unflattering candid shot in sight.

The grand ballroom was huge, white, and full of sparkling decorations. A live jazz band played tasteful standards under the conversation, with a few couples dancing and chatting on the dance floor. Expensive seafood was draped over a giant avalanche of ice on a long marble table, and a fountain burbled in the center of the room. Caterers, all in white, drifted from one side of the expansive room to the other, offering hors d'oeuvres to the millionaires and investors and Silicon Valley boy-geniuses. They were too busy invasively prodding and examining the new Miss Ordinarias, awestruck by their seeming so real.

It felt, all in all, more like a wedding reception than a donors' ball. A wedding reception at a gigantic doctor's office. This was both excellent branding work and a weird vibe that made Gideon even more nervous.

Ashbot didn't look fazed, because "fazed" was not a setting. She looked at him and smiled—he watched the glittery green makeup on her eyelids appear and disappear when she blinked. (They didn't need to blink, but the feature was added when the company realized the lack of blinking made people uncomfortable.)

"Why don't you go talk to them?" Gideon gestured toward the guys' dates, clustered in a tight circle in front of the bar.

"Okay!" She practically skipped away.

Gideon scanned the crowd. So, a black dress. It was impossible. They were on everybody, from eleven-year-old heiresses to seventy-year-old matrons. He could just give up. Maybe *she* would find *him*.

That's when he saw her.

He couldn't explain how he knew it was her, really, other than he just did. She was standing on the edge of the dance floor, her arms crossed, and she was staring at him without any subtlety. He began walking toward her, his heart pounding. She didn't move, didn't meet him halfway, and she wasn't smiling.

She just looked so *familiar* somehow, but the way déjà vu is familiar—it could be a real memory, or it could be that one of your synapses just fired weirdly for a second.

As he came closer, he saw she had brown hair, pinned back, and olive skin. She was sort of skinny-fat: skinny but not toned like Ashbot. Most of all, she stuck out. She didn't belong here. But instead of pitying her, or tattling to a security guard, Gideon immediately recognized himself in that.

Finally he reached her, and they faced each other.

"Who are you?" he asked apprehensively, then made a face. "God, this is so melodramatic."

She shrugged. "I'm Anonymous. Obviously."

"What's your real name?"

She continued glaring at him, ice-cold, and deadpanned: "You don't think my parents named me that?"

"If they did, you should call Social Services."

Bantering with her felt as natural as eating or sleeping. Weird—he was usually so quiet.

"So. Your dad's empire is doing well."

"Do you go to Pembrooke? Is that why I recognize you?"

Her mouth twisted in a sad smile.

"I've only been in your grade for, like, eight years. Sometimes in your class."

Gideon pushed on his temples, like it might shift his mind into place. Frustrated, he said, "I remember, but I . . . don't remember. Does that sound crazy?"

She shook her head, then glanced around them rapidly.

"We shouldn't talk here."

* * *

They walked briskly out of the industrial back door, her in the lead, and after five minutes wound up sitting on a curb just near the highway. It had rained, and the black pavement was strewn with shining puddles. The curb was damp, but the situation itself was too surreal for either of them to make "damp formal-wear ass" a priority right now.

"What's going on?"

She turned to him and took a breath, like she'd been preparing for this for months and knew she didn't have much time.

"They wiped your memories of me. And some . . . other things, which are also related to me. We were friends for a really, really long time. From when we were kids to when they found out."

"How would they *wipe* me? And they found out what? Just get to the point." Gideon was wondering if he should call 911 on this crazy girl. He was also beginning to notice that damp formal-wear ass right around now.

She halted and glared at him.

"Wait. First, can I just say, I can't believe you're doing what you're doing."

144

"Excuse me?"

"You're dating a Miss Ordinaria because someone told you to. You're hanging out with that human defect Jason Tous because someone told you to. When's the last time you made a decision by yourself?"

He was speechless.

"Exactly!" she yelled at him, emotion welling up in her eyes. Then she squashed it, and her tone was businesslike again. "If you came out as anti-Ordinaria, it would be huge! It would be, maybe, one of the only ways to stop this before it gets totally out of control."

"I don't get any of this. Just tell me, what don't I remember?"

She looked close to tears, which didn't make him feel that removed guilt he usually did when a girl cried. This time, he felt like *he* was close to tears.

"I'm sorry; I just don't remember!"

With wild eyes, she reached into her purse and pulled out a long screwdriver.

"You don't remember this?" she asked, her voice rising.

She raised her arm up as far as she could and slammed the screwdriver into her thigh.

Even before it came down, this thought popped into his head: *The screwdriver hits metal.*

As soon as that came back to him, with a click that felt like a brief migraine, he remembered everything. How they were drawn together as kids and didn't really know why. They'd spend every day together.

"You're Scarlett, aren't you?"

She nodded.

He remembered when she'd told him, crying, that her mom had simply stopped blinking. She said in that moment, the truth just *occurred* to her, even though she'd sort of known it all along. It was too crazy to believe. Gideon said maybe her mom had had a stroke. It sounded serious; her mom needed to go to the hospital.

She'd shaken her head slowly, looking around the room, eerily calm, then reached into his parents' junk drawer. Grabbed a screwdriver. Gideon had jumped up to stop her, but before he could she jammed it, hard, into her own leg.

The screwdriver hit metal.

They stood there, staring at each other.

"That's not possible. No."

"Wouldn't it make sense if we were drawn together for a reason?" she had asked. She told him—insisted, actually—to sneak a look into his parents' room late at night. *Maybe it won't be true,* she said, *but either way, you have to know, don't you?*

So that night at three A.M., he'd crept down the silent, echoing hall to the master bedroom to find out the truth. He'd cracked the door open, which thankfully didn't creak or moan—nothing in his house made noise—and peered in. His father was sound asleep in the king bed. His mother was standing up against the wall, her head tilted slightly down, shut off for the night to reactivate in the morning.

It was all coming back, even the memory wiping—shortly after he'd walked into their bedroom, his father had taken him to the family doctor, and then it all went blurry, his past reinvented.

Gideon shook his head vehemently.

"No. That's not possible. No way."

He heard himself echoing exactly what he'd said before. And he'd been wrong. She looked pained to make him so upset, but her voice was firm.

This was the reason rental Ordinarias were always sent across the country from renter to renter: Some visceral memory, like a moment, or even a sound, could bring it all back. Gideon's father had been very, very careful about it in business—but when it came to his own son, not careful enough.

"I'm half-Ordinaria," she said.

He closed his eyes.

She finished: "And so are you."

"How is that even possible?" he yelled.

"Brief, unfortunate flirtation with installing a reproductive system in the first-gen models. Only a handful of those models exist. And there are only two of us half-Ordinaria that I know of. We're freaks."

He hung his head, devastated. For a minute they just sat there, him processing and her waiting; the only noise was the rush of cars wetly speeding past them down the damp road.

Finally he said, "I'm sorry I hung out with those guys."

"Yeah," she said. "I'm sorry you did too."

"What can I do to make it up to you?"

She thought about it. Then she said, softly: "Don't forget again and leave me alone here."

Cerebrally, Gideon knew he should be wary of this girl who'd seemingly come out of nowhere. But in his heart, he knew that they were allies and needed each other to survive. At least for now.

He nodded, grave. "I promise."

They were both silent for a while.

"So then," he said, "you've just had that screwdriver in your purse for, like, years?"

"Yeah, pretty much."

He laughed a little. "That's weird."

She slowly turned to look at him, incredulous.

"*That's* weird?"

"I see your point."

Then they just sat there on the curb, all the shared history back, feeling as comfortable with each other as they'd felt uncomfortable with each other twenty minutes before, staring out at the highway that seemed to go nowhere.

"I hate it here," he whispered.

"Me too."

"You know, we don't actually have to do anything about this. I can pretend I still don't remember. Maybe I don't want to choose to be different."

She shook her head. "In that case, congratulations, because you're more like Jason Tous than you think you—"

Goddamn it, the doorbell's ringing.

"—are."

"Be there in a sec!" I yell. The response is a wordless shriek of fear, like a time-traveling Puritan who just saw her first car.

I click Post, then trudge to the door and open it to find Avery on the stoop, looking petrified, clutching four dresses on hangers underneath clear dry-cleaner cellophane and an industrial-sized makeup bag. She seems taller. It takes a second before I realize it's because she's not forced into crone position by a Jansport containing four math textbooks and the entire Western canon.

"I'm freaking out," she says in the measured tone of someone trying to stop freaking out. She walks past me inside, throws the dresses and makeup on the sofa, then sprawls out on her back on the floor.

"Fuck," she says. "Fuck, fuck, fuck, fuck."

"Okay, calm down."

"I don't know how to do this," she says in a monotone, staring blankly at the ceiling. "I'm overthinking it even though I know that's just making it worse."

"Dude, it's just a dance."

"I watched some YouTube tutorials on how to do a smoky eye, and now I look like a raccoon."

"Noooo! You look like Margot Tenenbaum!" I am an unconvincing liar.

She props herself up on her elbows and glares at me. "Don't undermine my intelligence."

"Okay, you're right, sorry. You look like a raccoon. A *pretty* raccoon."

Avery gets up and jokingly starts fake-going through the garbage, making raccoon noises, laughing. I double over, cracking up.

"Hang on a second. Dawn has makeup remover somewhere." I retreat to the bathroom and rummage around in the medicine cabinet until I find it.

Two barely defrosted shots of Dawn's freezer Svedka and an hour on Pinterest studying tutorials with names like "daytime smoky eye" and "~*~*prom hair~*~*" later, we still haven't managed to steer Avery's makeup away from ~*~*dumpster-diving varmint~*~**~.

"I need more of those pads!" she moans despondently, meaning the eye makeup–remover pads of Dawn's that we've been burning through. On my way to the bathroom to grab some more, I glance into my room, where the door is ajar, and see that the group chat is already on fire.

DavidaTheDeadly: so, the OC love triangle emerges . . . still think you could have made gidbot p. interesting from a character angle but whatev

WillianShipper2000: agree!!!!

DavidaTheDeadly: though it is nice to see that a (half-)

Ordinaria can think for herself.

xLoupxGaroux: Are you kidding me with this? Two words: Mary. Sue.

DavidaTheDeadly: gahhhhh. give it another installment at least!

xLoupxGaroux: Um, sweetie? 1) Half-breed. 2) High morals/ideals and terribly judgmental of others. 3) Looks fiercer than anybody else in eveningwear without trying. 4) Captivates main male protagonist without doing anything to earn it, really. Either our girl Scarface has been reading too much Ayn Rand (translation: any Ayn Rand) or this is a clear-cut Mary Sue issue.

Scarface: WAY HARSH, TAI. BTW: if you are 14 and read The Fountainhead you don't even notice the politics, it's really just a romance novel. Kind of a good one actually.

xLoupxGaroux: I'm gonna pretend you never said that. In fact, can you wipe my brain?

"Scar, where *are* you?!" Avery yells from the living room. "Sorry! Give me just a sec!"

WillianShipper2000: who is ayn rand even

WillianShipper2000: is she the one who has that advice column

xLoupxGaroux: Scar, I'm serious. Please brush up on the definition of MARY SUE on the "About Us/Rules" page and do a close read. I don't want to establish a pattern of lenience with this.

Scarface: dude . . . Do you really think she's a Mary Sue?

xLoupxGaroux: She's just too perfect. I want to see her be a real person. Not some idealistic fake paragon of virtue that is clearly a stand-in to make up for your terror of potentially having fun at a party.

Scarface: WTF?

xLoupxGaroux: Whole lot easier staying in and writing yourself brave instead of going out and BEING brave, is all I'm saying.

Scarface: What even are you

Scarface: OK, I guess that's valid.

WillianShipper2000: ok w8 bump to above question about Ayn Rand tho u guys.

xLoupxGaroux: Jesus. No, that's Ann Landers. Google it.

WillianShipper2000: No bc everything you tell me to Google is #BORING #OLD #PERSON #STUFF

xLoupxGaroux: If I have to know what "on fleek" means, you have to know some boring old person stuff.

Their banter lets me exit quietly and gracefully from the

chat, still smarting. Nauseated, I click on About Us in the upper left-hand corner and open the Mary Sue litmus test. It reads:

Hey, everybody! Everyone's encouraged to take risks in their fanfics, and for the most part, aside from hateful content or target harassment of anybody else on the board, anything goes. But it would be supercool to leave the Mary Sue stories—self-insertion into the Lycanthrope universe, based on the writer's wish fulfillment—at the door! Don't know if your original character is a Mary Sue? That's cool! Find out now.

IS YOUR OC A MARY SUE?

1) Does your character have the same name as you or a name that is a variant of yours, such as a nickname or different spelling?

Oh, god*damn it.*

2) Does your character look a lot like you?

3) Is your character the youngest in his/her given profession and also the most brilliant?

4) Does your character share strong opinions and beliefs with you?

5) Does he or she often state these opinions, argue with other characters about them, or try to win them over?

6) Does your character get listened to, followed, and respected more than his or her age, position, and experience would merit?

7) Is your character a hybrid of two races?

8) If so, is this hybrid race in any way "tragic" or "cursed"?

There's a loud knock at the door, and I dart through the living room to answer it, vaulting over the couch and scrambling nearly directly over Avery, who is wiping off her eye makeup as she warily eyes her phone, which is facedown on the coffee table.

"Who's here now, Gene Hackman?"

From outside: "It's Ashley!" More knocks. "Hell-ooooo?"

I summon my coldest glare at Avery, and she looks slightly guilty for a second but then throws her arms up with haplessly self-righteous attitude.

"She's good at this stuff! Okay? Get off my dick! Just be a normal human being for once. Please. I know you can do it." She wads up her third eye makeup–remover pad and tosses it into an empty coffee cup on the table. "I know things are weird between you guys, but she's not that bad, I swear."

I wave her off, taking pity on her, and open the door. Ashley's already in her dress for the dance, a cute black baby-doll-style cocktail dress that looks irritatingly perfect with her hair.

"Hey, Divider!" She smiles a big, toothy smile at me. "How excited are you for the dance!"

"Not going," I mutter, shuffling backward to let her in.

"Why? Too lame for you?"

"I've got plans later!" I sardonically try to match her bright tone.

"Whatcha doing?"

"I'm being executed by the state!"

Ashley seems not to hear me as she glows around my

apartment, idly picking things up, seeming to judge how much they cost, and putting them back down in ways that very clearly *show* how much she thinks they cost.

"It's cute here." She can't resist a passive-aggressive dig, adding, "*Cozy*."

"Ashley," shrieks Avery. "Help much?"

"Right. Yeah, totally. Okay, well. Oh—is that my dress?" Ashley stares at the navy dress Avery's wearing. Avery shrugs and tugs at its scalloped lace hem.

"Is that cool?"

"Of course. It looks hot on you! Very Kate Middy. Because, I mean"—she laughs, so lilting that you can almost picture the musical notes they'd use in closed-captioning—"I'm pretty obviously Pippa. Anyways, let's do this thing."

Ashley dumps the entire contents of her makeup bag onto the floor, and Avery slides off the sofa. They're both huddled on the carpet over the makeup like it's a fire keeping them warm. Ashley murmurs something to herself, then selects an eyeliner and leans in toward Ave until their identical strawberry blond heads are nearly touching. I feel a pang and wish, like I sometimes do, that Matilda and I were closer in age.

"Hey, Scarlett, have you got any nail polish remover?" Ashley waits a beat, then frowns a little and repeats, "Scarlett?"

I snap to attention, at this point totally used to her addressing me as Divider.

"Yeah, um, yeah, I'll get it."

As I head down the hall to Dawn's room, the familiar iPhone

text alert chimes from the living room. I nearly reach for my own phone anyway, a Pavlovian response.

"Oh God, he's texting me!" Avery yells from the other room.

"What did he say?" I yell back.

There's a pause as ostensibly she opens the text.

"*Sup!*" she shrieks, like the final girl in a horror movie.

Ashley works quickly. In twenty minutes, Avery has gone from ferret to fetching (which I'd watch the shit out of on Bravo). The makeup is flawless. The dress is classy but sexy. Her hair is simple but cute, just a few bobby pins drawing her bangs off her face. Mission accomplished.

"You look amazing," I assure her.

"Really?"

"Yes, totally."

"Thanks. Thank you. Sorry for . . ." She jerks her head, cockeyed, toward Ashley, who is checking her phone.

"Please, this is what I'm here for."

"Babe, we gotta go," Ashley interjects, a little more frozen over than she'd been just a second ago.

Avery nods stiffly, still looking incredibly nervous, picks up the little clutch she's chosen for the night, and heads for the door.

"Bye."

"See you, Divider," Ashley says flippantly as she waltzes out the front door. We had a good run with my God-given name for a minute there.

"Bye, have fun!"

Avery takes one step out the door, then she runs back and grabs my arm.

"You have to come with me."

"Ew. What? No."

"What if it's bad? Like, what if we have nothing to talk about, or dancing is awkward, or he tries to have sex with me?"

"Is he gonna?" I ask, startled.

"I have no idea! That's the point!"

Ashley dips backward through the doorway, grabbing the frame for support, and chirps, "You tell him *I* said you can't."

"But maybe I want to!"

Ashley gets an odd look on her face and says, "I had sex for the first time after a school dance when I 'maybe' wanted to, and it was awful."

Ave and I both look at her, taken aback. She shrugs, sort of sadly. The moment ends when Avery's phone chimes.

"Oh, it's him again."

She opens the text and reads it: "Where letter-R letter-U."

I roll my eyes. "Right out of Jane Austen."

"Please come, Scar. I'll owe you. I'll watch a whole season of *Lycanthrope* with you. I'll do your take-home math tests."

"You already do that."

She stops pleading and looks a little indignant. "Yeah. I do. So actually, you owe *me*."

I think of what Loup said about writing myself brave. Its accuracy is irritating. By staying inside and fantasizing instead of actually going out and doing something normal teenagers do, I accidentally Mary Sue'd myself to the first degree in front of my friends, writers that I respect. It's so humiliating. And it stops now.

"Okay," I say.

"Really?!" she squeals, jumping up and down.

"Yes."

Avery scoops up the makeup bag and tosses it to Ashley, who semi-begrudgingly catches it and comes back inside, shutting the door behind her.

"Your turn!"

chapter fifteen

MY DAD HAS THIS EXPRESSION: *If you're gonna be a bear, be a grizzly bear.* So I blew out my hair and borrowed an outfit from Dawn, and now I'm a grizzly bear in a short, tight red bandage dress that rides obscenely up my thighs when I get in the back of Ashley's car. I'd never admit it, but this dress makes me feel weirdly powerful and Kardashian-esque. It figures that I'd have to channel a totally different person in order to work up the nerve to go to this dance.

We pull into the class parking lot, and Ave and I both sort of take a second to regroup. Ashley reapplies her lipstick in the rearview mirror, visibly impatient to get inside already. Avery shakes her head in awe.

"I can't believe your boobs right now," she says.

"It's Dawn's bra."

In the interior rearview mirror, Ashley's green eyes creep

predatorily over to me, a spider crawling toward a fly.

"I didn't know Victoria's Secret had good clearance prices!" She shuts off the car.

A touching amount of time and effort has been spent making the gym look Halloween-y. Big black crepe paper covers the walls, and the backboards and basketball hoops are draped with cobwebs. I immediately zero in on Gideon—and so does Ashley, darting over in her tight black dress to back him (with him quite willing) into a corner. I watch them and hate myself for feeling like I'm at that first free fall on a roller coaster and my stomach has just dropped out of my body. He glances at me once, then again in a flickering up-and-down glance. Actually, I am either insane or I feel a lot of eyes on me.

"Oh my God, Scarlett, people are *staring* at you," says Avery.

I focus on the floor, yanking the bottom of my dress down.

Jason Tous saunters by with his little dude-cadre, reeking of Abercrombie Fierce. We glare at each other. I wonder whether he was even a little bit affected by what I said to him outside Ruth's house. It's hard to tell, since his expression is consistently at some unreadable early point on the Darwinian evolution chart.

Mike Neckekis appears from the refreshments table with two Solo cups of punch. He's wearing a nice gingham shirt and looks higher on the human-evolution chart than usual. He smiles at Avery and hands her a glass.

"Hey! You look really nice."

"You too," she says, seeming to relax a little, then lowers her voice: "Tell me this is alcoholic."

"Maybe a little," he says, and she makes a "score!" sign with her fist. He turns apologetically to me. "Oh, I'm sorry, I didn't get one for you. Wait a second." He disappears again to get a punch for me and returns with one. I sip and say thanks.

"So, like, you want to dance or something?" he asks Avery. She nods hesitantly and looks at me.

"Yeah, go! I mean, if nobody dances to the Black Eyed Peas, do they even exist? Just food for thought."

She laughs. "Okay. But listen, please don't feel weird that you came; you'll have fun. And you seriously look amazing. Everybody's staring at you."

I roll my eyes.

"I'll be back in a little bit."

The bleachers are reminiscent of Diane Arbus, smattered with a handful of homely Girl Geniuses and a couple of weird guys with pube-y facial hair who haven't had a growth spurt yet. As soon as I sit down way up on the highest bench, I feel a lot more like myself, in my natural habitat, but in keeping with today's little forum trauma, I'm not sure if that's a good thing or a bad thing.

Down below, my classmates are dancing or awkwardly milling around in same-sex groups. The guys seem aimless and doofy, trying to love-tap one another in the balls. The girls move with more of a purpose. Natalie Wetta and Jenna Salamon jokingly slow dance together. *We're all going to graduate soon, and go to college, and grow up, and get married*, I think, and realize with a start I've said *we* instead of *they*. Usually the only *we* is me and Avery, or me and the Were-heads. Or me and Gideon, before he outed himself as Lord of the Douche. I was so delusional to think he was above this popularity stuff.

I've tried to look everywhere except at Gideon and Ashley, but I'm a masochist, so I glance around for them. Ashley's nowhere to be found, and hearing a few thuds of dress shoes on the bleachers, I realize Gideon's climbing up toward me. I am still mad at him, no matter how cute he looks.

This is the part where I am supposed to be a sparkling, vindictive angel of revenge whose cutting remarks make him feel like shit.

"I like your shoes," I blurt.

He glances down at them. "Oh. Thanks." Then he sits next to me, leaning a little bit forward with his hands on his knees, staring straight out at the dance floor like he's intentionally trying not to look at me.

"So did you get to the Sam Kieth illustrated editions?"

I don't say anything. I freeze helplessly, torn between wanting to yell at him about his cisgender white male sense of entitlement and whisper to him that he smells like pine needles and dreams.

"It, um, was really stupid, what I did."

He has now given me permission to go with option one.

"It was pretty spectacularly stupid, yeah."

"I didn't know who lived there. Not that that's better, but if I knew it was, like, an old lady by herself—and that you knew her—then I might not have . . ." He trails off. "I totally forgot you lived in that neighborhood."

"Well, I do."

"Can you, um, tell her I'm sorry? For me?"

"I already told her."

"Did you?"

"Yeah, I told her I was sorry I go to school with a bunch of idiots who ruined her garden, and that people do really shitty things to fit in without thinking about it at all. And that I ever thought for a split second that you were cool."

He looks stunned, which makes me even angrier, because it's obvious that he chooses to hang out with girls who never tell him off and just let him get away with anything. And I'm so, so annoyed at myself for caring about it.

He turns toward me, his nose crinkled up with irritation, as if I'm being An Emotional Girl™ and missing some major piece of information that makes him not an utter ass.

"Scarlett," he says.

"What?"

He shakes his head, one side of his mouth twisting in kind of an embarrassed smile.

"The only reason I went with them in the first place was because you said I had no friends."

He sighs. Then he gets up and walks back down to the dance floor.

That's bullshit, I think. Maybe it was partly what I said, but he loves having baller status at school. It's so unfair—I put on the dress, came to the dance, and actually tried, and nothing worked out the way I wanted it to. I should have known that coming was a stupid idea.

I track down Avery and tell her I'm gonna go.

"No! Why? Did Gideon say something to you?"

"Yeah, but that's not why. I'm tired. I'm in a shitty mood. I've been sucking in my stomach for, like, two hours. I need to go home."

"Come dance with us."

I glance warily at Mike, who nods and smiles in a seemingly genuine way. I really don't want some bullshit charity third-wheel routine.

"Okay. I'll need some more punch."

Three Solo cups later, I'm nice and tipsy enough to non-self-consciously dance with Avery in sort of a performative, faux-dirty way that Mike and some other boys nearby who've never looked twice at us seem to appreciate. But we're totally ignoring them. We don't usually act like this. Our friendship isn't really very affectionate or physically silly. Most of the time we sit kind of far away from each other and banter because we're both weird and trapped in our own heads and

SCARLETT EPSTEIN HATES IT HERE

uncomfortable with touchy-feely stuff. Like two brains in a jar.
But it's surprisingly fun to just let go.

The Fray comes on, a slow song, and Mike and Avery dance
as I go get more punch. Unexpectedly, as I'm ladling punch
into my cup, my eyes start swimming with tears. At the Fray.
I'm obviously losing it. Or I'm just turning into Dawn, who
full-body sobs during Super Bowl commercials about Sprint
"framily" plans. It was only a matter of time.

Gideon and Ashley slow dance, but over her shoulder, he's
looking at me. His expression looks studiously blank, like it
used to when he was troubled about something, trying to parse
out a jumble of thoughts in his head, but who knows what it
means now? I wish he'd stop. *Yes, I'm standing alone, as usual. Gawk
at me all you'd like when I'm dead and stuffed and posed in the Museum
of Natural History as Girl Standing by Herself.*

Careful what you wish for, though: He stops looking at me
when Ashley pulls him down toward her, tangling her fingers in
his slightly-too-long dark hair forever brushing his collar, and
they kiss. And I die a little.

They're still kissing when I leave.

chapter sixteen

I'M STARTING TO GET WHY Ruth was surprisingly nonchalant in the wake of Gardenpocalypse. The flowers are nice, but it's the actual gardening part that's cathartic. You're basically brawling with dirt. I especially need to blow off steam because the BNFs—and other people in the fandom—are starting to write response fics about Gideon and Ashbot and Scarlett, which is simultaneously incredibly cool and more than a little weird. As I sweat it out in shitty dad-style jeans with my hair pulled up in a topknot, getting the November tulip bulbs started, I begin to feel a little better.

"So?"

"Yes?"

"Do you forgive him?" asks Ruth, her tone implying that I'm a complete idiot.

"What do you mean? You're the one he apologized to."

The wind blows Ruth's overpowering weed smoke toward me, and I cough. "God."

"He's obviously apologizing to *you*. He doesn't know me from Adam."

"I'm not the one he was making out with on the dance floor."

"You could've been."

"You mean if I'd just acted like everything was totally fine? Like you said, I don't know how to be fake." My raking becomes harder and more vicious. "And I learned my lesson. I'm never going to another dance again. Guest starring in one episode of *The Young and the Vacant* was enough for me."

Maybe I had a sliver, like, a *modicum* of fun. But there's no way I'd tell her that.

Ruth shakes her head. "You're so angry all the time. Aren't you tired?"

"I'm kidding. I mean, I won't go to another dance, but I'm mostly joking."

"That's what's angry, the jokes."

I wipe the sweat off my forehead with the back of my garden glove, exasperated.

"How about you try to analyze me when you're *not* completely stoned."

"Sure, make an appointment for the twelfth of never."

I snort. Ruth picks up expressions—what she'd call, offensively, "street"—from Ave and me that she uses wrong half the time and dead-on perfectly the other half. I'm about to respond to her when I realize she's looking past me, smiling. A voice pipes up from behind me.

"Scarlett?"

I turn. Gideon's standing hesitantly at the edge of the garden, holding a potted orchid.

"Oh, wow." He blinks. "Those are some serious Jerry Seinfeld pants."

"Hello, Newman."

"I was wondering if you'd mind if I, like, helped you."

The surprise and weirdness of him being there makes me docile. I nod. "Okay."

Ruth clears her throat.

"I think I'm gonna take a nap."

Gideon looks straight at her and says supersincerely, "I'm really sorry I did this to your garden."

"Thank you. You're a nice boy," she replies without her usual saltiness—instead, like a kindly grandma. Then she goes inside. Gideon points toward the door with a perplexed smile.

"Um, was she just smoking weed?"

"Yep."

He nods, impressed, and says mildly, "Right on."

"Your clothes are going to get dirty," I warn him.

"That's cool."

"So . . . um, yeah." I gesture to the tools stacked up against the side of the porch. "Grab a hoe."

"There's nothing I'd rather do," he jokes.

"I figured. You're kind of a rake."

He nods seriously. "Good for you, calling a spade a spade."

I laugh, surprised, then narrow my eyes and fake-glare suspiciously at him. He smiles back. We're flirting, I think. It's sort of a dogs-circling-each-other flirt. He seems to be sizing it up the same way I am.

Then he says, "A hot Jerry Seinfeld is what I meant."

I might pass out. Instead I say, hopefully coolly: "Right. Obviously."

I assign him one particular square of the garden, and we work in silence for a while. He starts sweating and takes his fleece off, underneath which is a white T-shirt that fits him perfectly, and I pretend not to notice.

"Remember that time you said I didn't have friends?" he asks, his tone light and joking but a little wounded.

"I didn't really mean it that way."

"I know. But, like, how would you know if I even did? Besides them, I'm, um . . . I take classes in the city at this comedy place? Upright Citizens Brigade? That's where my best friends are, really."

My heart twists a little at his nervous uptalk.

"Yeah, of course. Avery and I try to go every few weeks. I've seen a lot of shows there."

"Really?" He's relieved and, judging by the sudden grin, delighted. "That's cool! And, like . . . most of your friends are on the Internet, right?"

He doesn't sound judgmental, just curious. Ashley must've told him.

"Um, when you say it like that, it sounds pretty creepy. But, yeah, some of them."

"What do you talk about with them?"

"*Lycanthrope High*, obviously."

"But the show's over. So what about now?"

I begin to feel the blood rush out of my head, the start of a small panic attack. *Right now we're discussing the speculative fiction I'm writing about you and your maybe-girlfriend.*

"Nothing important," I say.

He nods.

"And I hang out with people here, too. I have hang partners," I add.

"Well, there's Ashley's sister," he says, teasing.

"Yeah."

"And there's . . ." He pretends to think. "An old woman."

I laugh again, my anxiety dissipating.

"Seriously, though, I'm not saying that's a bad thing. I mostly hang out with other kids in my improv class. We just get along really well. School isn't really where most of my friends are."

"Well!" I say brightly, trying not to come off too caustic. "You really seem to be spreading your wings this year, you li'l social butterfly."

"Yeah. I know." His response is weirdly ambivalent, and he hangs his head a little. Good! He should. Or: I like him, and he shouldn't. Depends on what precise second you ask me.

"You're like the boy *She's All That*," I say. "The glasses come off, and bam."

"Yeah, I've got that little red dress, too." He shovels dirt over a bulb, then goes: "Wait, no, that's you."

I blush. Then I surprise myself by asking, with pure curiosity: "How does it feel?"

"How does what feel?"

"To be popular."

He scoffs. "I'm not p—"

"Shut up. Don't do that bullshit; we'll all be dead someday, and you'll have wasted time."

He stands, thoughtful, for a moment.

"Weird," he says. Then admits, "Good."

I nod and wait for him to elaborate. Mostly for him to admit to aiding Jason and co. in their reign of terror. He doesn't.

Instead, he asks, "How does it feel to be smart?"

"Um, hello. Thirty-seven. A score not found in nature. You're asking the wrong person."

He shakes his head.

"I don't mean good in school. You're the smartest person I know."

"Not really," I mumble, uncomfortable.

"I've always thought . . ." He blushes. "Like, there's one thing you're really, really good at, but you don't talk about it or tell anybody. I've always thought you were hiding some giant thing."

Always thought. My face burns. *He thinks about me.* For some reason, I feel exposed and immediately want to shock him or put him off as much as possible.

So I say, "It's my giant cock."

"Very funny."

"My huge, veiny monster cock. It's incredibly unwieldy."

"Scarlett," he says, sort of chastising, looking straight at me.

My face burns like I'm divulging some enormous shameful secret. "I like writing."

"Like poetry?"

"*God* no."

"Then what?"

"I don't know. Stories, I guess. Maybe . . . novels? I hate how that sounds, though. I don't know. Let's not talk about it."

"Okay."

We dig in silence some more, until he says: "So are we going to plant this Georgia O'Keeffe steez, or, like . . ."

"Totally, bring that vagina flower over here."

His turn to blush. He brings it over, and we plant it together, like some weird on-the-nose sex metaphor. I wonder if he's slept with Ashley. As if he can tell what I'm thinking, he gives me a frustratingly inconclusive nonanswer.

"We're not official. Ashley and me, I mean."

"Like, not BF-GF."

"Definitively. No. Not."

"What do you want me to do with that information, exactly?"

He shrugs. Guys are so unfair. One shrug, and I'm lying in bed that night replaying the whole scene, every look he shot me, feeling a weird and very real glow I've never really felt before.

So I do what I always do when I have two feelings that are pulling me in opposite directions: I write it for the BNFs.

Basically the exact conversation Gideon and I had in the garden, albeit continuing the Ordinaria metaphor I've built into the previous installments.

As I hit Post, I felt weirdly exposed, like all my sentences were stripped of their woolen layers and stood there naked, unprepared for the elements.

But the BNFs had asked for it. Instead of lofty fights about morals or ideals, they seemed to want me to write . . . what happened, and how I felt about it. That is, how Scarlett felt about it. I mean, *that* Scarlett. Or—you know what I mean.

> **xLoupxGaroux: Good stuff.**
>
> **DavidaTheDeadly: all right, i'm coming around on this pairing. there's def some meaty stuff here.**
>
> **WillianShipper2000: idk i don't really see sideon . . .**
>
> **DavidaTheDeadly: it's all about the character-building now! ashbot still has the furthest to go . . . but that's by design, clearly. i mean it's all there on her twitter**
>
> **Scarface: wait what twitter?**
>
> **DavidaTheDeadly: Ashbot's twitter, isn't it you?**
>
> **Scarface: no . . .**
>
> **DavidaTheDeadly: whoa i guess it's a stan. it has like 50 followers.**
>
> **MorwennaWraith: Here's the problem: People keep**

asking for Sideon fanart, but Scarlett doesn't sound that pretty

Scarface: WTF

DavidaTheDeadly: dude OTPs aren't determined by "who's the hottest person"—just look at greg and becca. john, like scarface, is a feminist. he very well would want gideon to end up with whoever was the best on the *inside.*

Scarface: haha guys, she's not like

Scarface: an absolute gnarled crone who lives in a hole but manages to get by because of her amazing personality

Scarface: she's like . . . okay-looking and has a pretty good personality

Scarface: i think

xNorthStarx: Hi! Longtime lurker, first-time poster here. Really into this chapter. But . . . does Ashbot know about any of this? She may not have female intuition, but she has a built-in GPS, which is sort of the same thing. If Ashbot and Gideon have been hooking up and he hasn't mentioned this, he's kind of being a dick.

Werehead66: Hi, same, never posted here before. Sideon OBVIOUSLY makes more sense. They obviously have a connection, plus a pretty epic backstory. Besides,

I don't know if Gideon's really beholden to Ashbot! I think he's just going with the flow.

Scarface: I mean maybe he hasn't hooked up with her though

WillianShipper2000: yea, who's to say? ppl wait to have sex for all kinds of reasons

xLoupxGaroux: Willian, babygirl, we know your deal. But what most teenagers do at afterprom isn't getting a hamburger with your dad after the Purity Ball.

Willian goes to one of those schools where "sex ed" is when the health teacher passes an unwrapped Peppermint Pattie around the classroom, finally grosses out a student by asking him to eat it, and compares it to a girl who won't wait until marriage.

xNorthStarx: I've been sending my friends Ordinaria chapters and one of them was pretty indignant about the emotional cheating.

xLoupxGaroux: "Emotional cheating??" God, that is such a hetero conceit I want to vom.

xNorthStarx: Anyway, my friends want more! And they're not even Lycanthrope fans.

Werehead66: I just want Gideon to be HONEST with both of them. No more of this ambiguity. You know??

The longer he drags this out, the easier he is to dislike. You can't have your cake and eat it too, you know?

Scarface: What a weird idiom though because what else can you do with cake? But I get what you mean. Believe me.

Werehead66: John St. Clair only waited two seasons to hook William and Gillian up. Enough with the will-they-or-won't-they, I want a true love scene.

xLoupxGaroux: OK, fine. If I have to live vicariously through the shipping of a straight couple, I'll do it. Just consummate one of them already.

WillianShipper2000: maybe he'll realize ashbot is the ONE (and also prettier but I know i know it doesn't matter because #feminism)

Werehead66: No way! #Sideon-shipper for life!

xNorthStarx: IDK, guys, I'm kind of still #Gidbot.

WillianShipper2000: hell yeeeeeaaaa

xLoupxGaroux: I'm gonna need more chapters

DavidaTheDeadly: Same.

xNorthStarx: SAME.

chapter seventeen

USUALLY I'D RATHER BE BURIED ALIVE as the sacrificial virgin in an Aztec tomb than wake up for school on Monday. This morning, though, I wake up feeling almost happy to head to homeroom with damp hair at seven forty-five A.M. sharp, like I've just emerged from Dawn's Pinterest board of inspirational quotes.

Gideon and I were up late, texting back and forth about *Lycanthrope High* graphic novels. He's supposed to lend me the last couple of Sam Kieth installments, which were sold out at the comic book store. I ended up picking up some other stuff of his. (Side note: His other stuff is the shit too.)

As I'm toasting an English muffin in the kitchen, Dawn trudges out of her bedroom, picking leftover crusty mascara off her lashes. She walks by me to get a plate; her pores smell like a whiskey distillery.

"Shut up and sit down, young lady," she croaks. "I'll finish breakfast."

After a rough night out, she always feels guilty and goes all Attack of the Mom on me. (See: the only time she ever says things like "young lady.")

"Already done." I toss a piping hot muffin onto my plate. I butter it as she hollows out hers with a fork. Her carb-calories fear makes her turn everything into a bread bowl.

"Don't forget, we're having dinner with Brian tonight."

I slump forward onto the table. "Nooooo."

"I know it'll be hellish for you," she says faux-sympathetically, "but at least you have Friday to look forward to."

"Friday? What's Friday?"

"Your dad's book party."

I brighten instantly—an already awesome week has improved exponentially. I was so wrapped up in the Gideon drama that I'd totally forgotten that his launch was this week.

"We discussed it, and he said you should spend the weekend with them in Brooklyn and come back Sunday night."

"Okay!"

I carry my plate over to the sink, musing, "I didn't even know you still talked."

"Well, we do."

"What could you possibly have to say to each other?"

"We *were* married for twelve years, Scar." I wait. She shrugs. "And he sometimes calls me when he's not sure how to take care of the baby."

"The blind leading the blind, huh?"

She jokingly glares at me, then says, "I don't know. I think I did okay."

"Give me time! Soon I can be charged as an adult."

She checks her iPhone. "It's eight ten. Go get an education."

I'm shoving books in my locker hastily before the bell rings when Avery rushes up to me, uncharacteristically late. I suddenly understand where the phrase "a spring in her step" comes from. She's practically Riverdancing.

"Hiii," she chirps.

"Who put meth in your Cheerios?"

"Not funny, meth is a serious problem, Mike and I almost did it last night," she says in one breath.

"Whoa. What? Really?"

She nods about fifty times.

"How was it?"

She beams and raises her eyebrows a few times, like a small overachieving Groucho Marx.

"*Almost*, though? Okay, like, what base, exactly?"

"Well, I did some research on this—"

"God, of course you did; go on."

"And there's actually not a standardized definition of bases. It's actually a really inefficient nonunified language of sexual activity. Like, some people think first base is holding hands, and some people think first-base is kissing, and some people think it's *tongue* kissing—"

"See also: the chase, cut to."

"I mean, he, like, you know."

She makes a brisk series of hand gestures that culminate in one large TMI. (I'm sparing you.)

"Okay. I see. Wow. Visuals. Got it."

"It was good, though. I was really scared at first. But he was really nice. I think he's done it before!" she says gleefully, then looks a little bit annoyed, then looks gleeful again.

"Probably not, like, five minutes before," I reassure her. "So, like . . . how do you feel?"

"I think . . . different, sort of. Not in any specific way. Just overall," she sighs, then she gives me this look. It's new and I don't like it. Sort of, *Two roads diverged in a wood, mine is normal, but I hope you can be happy for me even though you are Miss Havisham.*

"Anyway, what's going on with me is," I say, like she just asked me, "Gideon and I were talking last night about comics."

"Cool."

I can tell that she thinks I'm still playing in the minor leagues. Which I guess I am, but I'm still pretty psyched about it. To be honest, thinking about the mechanics of actually hooking up with somebody, even Gideon, makes me next-level anxious.

"So . . . what else?"

"What else? He's gonna lend me some comics."

She nods and waits like there's more. I shrug.

"And then he's going to make passionate love to me on Mr. Radford's desk. What do you want?"

"I just think you should do something."

"I am doing things!"

"Not really. You're, like, being receptive to the things *he's* doing. I think *Lycanthrope High* brainwashed you."

I laugh in disbelief. "What?"

"One, like . . . cryptic, brooding look, or ambiguous sentence, and you're set for, like, six months. You're like a squirrel, and tiny little signals are the nut, and you go store it away forever."

"As opposed to . . .?"

"Eating the nut!" she yells just a little too loud.

"I didn't want to have to go here, but I really don't need to play Six Degrees of Gideon's Bacon with your sister." I slam my locker shut for emphasis. She holds her hands up in surrender.

"Dude. Scar, I swear, I don't know what's even happening with them."

"Really? 'Cause you take more than enough notes in health, so I think you do."

"The thing is, you just"—she stops, then rolls her eyes—"you always just assume the worst."

"Well, usually I'm right. So."

I start off down the hall, then turn around and yell: "Mazel on becoming a woman, sort of!"

I see her stop, freeze in embarrassment, and then continue walking like she didn't hear me.

I can't concentrate on classes, which is pretty standard for me, but for a different and more butterfly-stomach-inducing reason than usual. AP English is only every other day, so the first time I'll see Gideon this afternoon is in the cafeteria.

He's sitting with Ashley, Natalia, and a bunch of the large

guys who usually buzz around their hive, including Jason Tous and the other ones who wrecked Ruth's garden. After I put my tray down at the Girl Genius table, I walk over there and tap him on the shoulder. He half turns.

"Hey! Did you bring the comics for me?"

Ashley glances up at me, smiles, and puts her hand on Gideon's arm.

"Hey, Divider!" she chirps.

"What comics?" asks Gideon.

"Like . . . you know, from when we were talking last night?"

"Oh. Yeah, I forgot, I guess."

"I like your shirt!" She absently rubs Gideon's arm. "I had one like that last year. I gave it to Goodwill."

Jason Tous, meanwhile, seems to be bypassing the passive-aggressive remarks and going straight to the glare.

"You narc on anybody lately?" Jason asks me.

I feel the blood drain out of my face. "No," I say stupidly.

"Really?" asks Dylan. "You seem like you like it. The same way you like running around acting like a big butch lesbian."

I look at Gideon. He says nothing—just stares down at his Tater Tots like they're an ancient rune to decode.

"You're right, Dylan. I'm a big butch lesbian narc. Gosh, it feels great to stop living a lie. You should try it," I say, then turn to Jason. "Don't you see how he looks at you?"

"What the—nah, dude," Jason sputters.

"Homophobics are often self-hating. You'd probably be a lot happier if you stopped terrorizing old ladies and just went full *Modern Family*," I say. "Enjoy the tots."

I turn and start walking away, humiliated that I thought Gideon would follow through on anything he said to me when we were alone, outside of school, in the safe bubble of late-night texts. I hate myself even more when I glance back on the off chance that he's trailing behind me. No dice.

Avery is sympathetic to my situation when I return to the Girl Genius table and explain it. However, her version of counsel is trying to distract me by reading fun facts from the "baseball metaphors for sex" Wikipedia page, and it makes me want to take a Silkwood shower.

So I bail on lunch and try to go write in the library, but the arc of the Ordinaria is all off now, and I don't get anything done—just a few false starts, somewhere between what I'd written before and the last chapter I'd written, that end up in the trash file on my laptop. Which is annoying, because I could use the group's support now more than ever.

Dinner with Dawn's latest Match.com rando is worse than I thought it would be. Rather than at the very least removing one aspect of the awkward intimacy of this meal, he's bringing over the fixings and, for the first time basically ever, we're *making* dinner. At home.

Dawn darts around anxiously, throwing out old bills and cleaning invoices scattered around the counter, checking her hair.

"Scar, get off the computer."

I reluctantly close my laptop.

"Go put on something nice, please."

She means something that isn't Dad's. I tug at his oversized Rolling Stones tee, tenting comfortably on me. "This isn't nice?"

"Now."

Brian's car crunches into the driveway. As soon as I watch him getting out of the car from the window, I begin the official evaluation. It always starts here. If it didn't, I would never have caught that one dude who told Dawn he had no kids surreptitiously hiding a pink-and-black car seat in his trunk.

I fold my arms as I do some initial scrutinizing from afar. Dawn's darting around the kitchen making some unnecessary last-minute tweaks, like moving the salt shaker a quarter of an inch to the right.

"What is that, a Fiat?"

Dawn barely hears me, too busy glancing in the full-length mirror and smoothing down her dark blue pencil skirt. I told her to pick something for me to wear to save us the trouble of creating a discarded-clothing snowstorm in my room, so she picked a dress my grandma handmade for her when she was my age, and now I look like a Mexican place mat.

"Audi," Dawn mumbles, preoccupied.

Good choice. Nice, but not obnoxious. (In the past few years of Dawn's dating life, we've both become attuned to car brands the way some people really care about the zodiac signs of their dates. Since middle-aged guys all basically dress the same, it's the only real snap judgment you can make.)

This guy, though? Well, at least he isn't bald. His head's just shaved, which is a surprisingly good look for him. Square jaw. Weird, wispy blond eyebrows that are barely visible. He's tall and lanky, and his suit is clearly expensive but not showy about it.

"Not bad," I say, somewhat begrudgingly.

He looks up, sees me in the window, and jumps a little. Good. Let him think I'm a weird Mexican place mat ghost. Dawn strikes a match to another tea light.

"Oh, good, I didn't think there were enough tea lights," I say.

Every time Dawn didn't know what to do with her hands, she lit another tea light, so now there are approximately 2,523 tea lights glowing in the living room.

I turn away from the window, frowning at her a little. "You know, if you're still nervous about this guy after this long, I'm not sure that's a good sign."

"I'm not nervous about him. I'm nervous *for* him."

"Why?"

She looks at me like it's obvious.

"I'm nervous you'll eat him alive."

Then we run down to help Brian carry the groceries up from the car.

I am steeling myself for the first interaction, which is always the worst and consistently determines the rest of the evening. I just hope he doesn't say, "Howdy, girlfriend" or tell me I look "just like [my] mother" while staring at my boobs, like some of Dawn's greatest hits.

"Hey," he says. He shakes my hand a little bit like I'm a dude from the office. "I'm Brian."

All right, that's passable.

As he and Dawn laugh together, shouldering the Whole Foods totes, it is obvious to me that there's way more food than is necessary for just one dinner. Clearly, he thinks we're in need or something.

"There are only three of us," I point out, bristling. He could at least halfheartedly try to hide the charity.

"Oh, I dunno. I just saw a pretty romantic movie where someone eats more than they need to." He shrugs, smiling at Dawn. "I guess it got me carried away."

I roll my eyes.

"Ever seen *Se7en*?" he asks.

I laugh. Like, out loud. Then I think: *Holy shit. This guy might not be the worst.*

In fact, the evening is more than a few notches above painless, which makes it about a hundred times better than any other one of these. Finally, this isn't another asshole with a nice car, another crying jag and sauvignon blanc bender, another time Dawn got her hopes up for nothing. And maybe a couple of times I did too.

I sit on the couch and watch them sear some chicken breasts together, Brian occasionally throwing me a question about school.

"Let me save you time," I say from the sofa, where I am sprawled channel surfing. "Eleventh grade, two point nine GPA, hate it."

"Scarlett, turn off the TV and be helpful, please," says Dawn. I do not listen.

"You ever see *Shawshank Redemption*?" asks Brian.

"Yep."

"Have you considered tunneling yourself out over a period of twenty years or so?"

"Oh," I laugh dryly. "I thought you were gonna ask if I've considered hanging myself."

They both stop and look at me. The only noise is sizzling chicken and the dense buzz of awkwardness.

"You know, the guy who gets out? He hangs himself? Never mind."

"I do remember. And, nah, I'd just stick with tunneling."

"Noted."

"Okay, so . . ." Brian pretends to jot something down. "Caustic stepdaughter. I can deal with that."

Dawn laughs and nudges him playfully with her hip, looking happier than I've seen her in a long time. (*Stepdaughter!!!* I know she's thinking, with multiple exclamation points, in that brain of hers that probably looks like a Buzzfeed list of the best kitten GIFs.)

It's funny. This whole time I thought I hated Dawn's boyfriends because she seemed to spend more time dating them than she did with me, but now I realize I just hated them because I never saw them make her look like that.

chapter eighteen

I FIND RUTH SITTING in the dirty white lawn chair on
her patio, smoking her customary joint, totally engrossed in a
book. Even in the nice weather, she's still in her uniform of
a crisp white dress shirt and wool trousers, with the small
addition of cat-eye sunglasses. She lowers them down her nose
and stares at me.

"You look bummed, lady," she says.

"I'm a little bummed."

"You want a beer?"

"I'm okay, thanks."

"I'm gonna get a beer."

She goes in, then comes back out with a giant forty-ounce, one
of those brands you see being swigged from a brown bag mostly
by burnout kids whose social lives revolve around parking lots.

She cracks it open.

"What happened?"

"Nothing. I don't know. Gideon's been ignoring me."

"Yeah." She pauses thoughtfully and kicks out her thin legs. "He didn't talk to you at school when other people were around?"

Mildly surprised, I reply, "Yeah."

She nods and twists her mouth sympathetically, saying nothing.

"Well?" I prompt.

"Well, what?"

"Don't you have some kind of, like"—I am about to say *wisdom*, but I remember just in time that it's her least favorite word—"crazy story about how you once slept with Francis Ford Coppola and learned something? I could use some levity."

"Nope," she says simply.

"Wow. The one time I actually ask for TMI."

"A story! Okay. I can give you a story. So. I know this is a pretty big bomb to drop on you, but . . . I was your age once."

"Really? This whole time I thought you sprang from Zeus's head as an AARP member."

"Well. I grew up in a really small town in rural Pennsylvania. My father died when I was six. He had a heart attack in bed one night, and my mother woke up and found him next to her cold. Did I ever tell you this?"

I shake my head. She sighs.

"Anyway. After that, my mom got real religious, thought God had punished her for not being a better Christian. I stopped going to church around fifteen. She would get royally pissed at me, take out her belt, the whole thing."

I wince.

"Around this time, a new family moved to town. They were the first, and the only, black family in our neighborhood. They became the subject of a lot of gossip, especially in my momma's church. The funny thing was, they were Christians too—they were Baptists and went to a church that seemed much more fun. And if you're having fun, Catholics pretty much assume you're a bad Christian.

"Anyway, they had a son my age, and unfortunately for him he got sent to my high school, which was religious Catholic. So he got a lot of shit from the other kids, obviously, about looking different, and cracks about how much the tax was on his folks, dumb stuff like that. I was getting some shit too at the time from kids at school, mostly for showing up drunk and running with what they thought was a bad crowd. I was considered . . . you know. I don't know what they'd call it."

"A bad influence?" I ask, and sigh quietly.

She nods.

"But I noticed him and started watching him. He wasn't like anybody else and not just because he wasn't white. He was thoughtful and quiet, and he'd read all the time, not for school but for fun. Mostly books about philosophy, or huge fantasy novels like *The Lord of the Rings*. So one day I went up to him when he was sitting on the bleachers reading during a pep rally, and we started talking.

"His name was Leon. He hated school like I did, but his method was more to just put his head down and get through it so he could make his parents proud. I really admired him. We couldn't spend time together in school, because people would talk—but we started taking long walks, hanging out whenever we could. He encouraged me to pay more attention. He said I was smart and I could have an amazing life if I stopped trying to waste it. I think part of him was mad at me, probably—he had to work twice as hard to get to where he wanted to go, and here was this white girl, not even using her instant pass.

"People had said that to me ever since I started cutting class and skipping church, but I'd never listened because they were . . . well, horrible people." Ruth chuckled. "But Leon didn't mean it in a preachy way. He said it very matter-of-factly. And I thought about it. I started doing better in school. We fit together, in some odd way, after growing up not fitting anywhere else. His family had me over for dinner, and they were really sweet, totally accepted me at their dinner table with no questions or judgment. He mentioned once that he could marry whomever he chose. They just wanted him to be happy. Which, again, considering I'd had my mother buzzing in my ear this whole time about what God approved of and what He didn't, seemed a whole lot more Christian to me than what I'd been raised to think like. So I really, really liked his parents, probably I was even a little jealous.

"One afternoon, some nosy woman from church saw us walking back from school and told my mother. When I got home, she screamed that if I wasn't going to hell anyway for being disobedient and doubting the Lord's way, I certainly would if I was splitting a chocolate malt with some black boy right under her and God's nose. I said the Bible preaches tolerance, and quoted Ephesians 4:32: 'Be kind to one another, tenderhearted, forgiving one another, as God in Christ forgave you.' After that, she really went nuts. Beat the shit out of me."

Ruth swigs her beer as I wait, spellbound. She has never told me a story this way, staring out at the lawn and speaking in a low, flat voice, like more of her energy is required to pull it out of her memory than to deliver it in an engaging way. I register distantly that my phone's vibrating, but I don't pick it up.

"But nobody could keep Leon and me apart, no matter how hard my mother beat me or how many rocks the kids at school threw at us when we'd leave together, him carrying my schoolbooks. We were inseparable. We graduated—him with honors, me just barely—and left town together. We never went back."

She stops talking. My phone buzzes again. I don't even look at it; I'm too enthralled. It sounds like a Nicholas Sparks movie, for God's sake.

"And?" I urge her.

"What do you mean, *and*?"

"Like . . . did you fall in love? Get married? What happened?"

Ruth snorts. "Nothing!"

I must look incredibly confused because then she nearly doubles over, her thin frame shaking with laughter.

"Scarlett, I'm *gay*."

I almost fall off the bench.

"What?!"

"Gosh, I thought it's been obvious all these years. Did you not know?"

"No! I mean, it's not a big deal, obviously. I'm just surprised because—I mean, that is an epic story! What's the point of it all, then?!"

"The point is, the outcome's *not* the point. We got out of our shitty town and went to New York together. We did everything we planned to do."

I nod, feeling my eyes get embarrassingly misty.

She sighs, as if she thinks everything she's about to say is something that's going in one of my ears and out the other, and says, "The best parts of life aren't clear-cut or obvious—they don't have neat endings. I know it's your inclination to skip to the end, but you can't just focus on how it's all gonna turn out."

I nod.

"Anyway, he married a really amazing, funny woman he met in New York, and we stayed in touch until he passed away. I'm still in touch with his widow, although we're both getting up there, and it's harder to travel." She glances upward for a second, and I wonder if she's about to cry. Instead, she lets out a sharp little laugh and admits, "To be honest, I'm pretty tired of saying goodbye to people."

I'm not sure how to respond. Finally, I ask, "How come you're telling me all this now?"

"Because I'm baked," she says. I laugh, relieved she's given me an excuse to.

It's hard to feel like I have nothing to offer, when usually I can joke about something and make it all better. I don't wish she hadn't told me, because I feel closer to her than I ever have, but it's left me feeling heavy, like I have an emotional hangover that no greasy breakfast sandwich can cure.

chapter nineteen

DAD'S BOOK PARTY is tonight. If I had the balls, I'd show up with a polka-dot kerchief full of belongings on a stick and begin a scrappy new life on the mean streets of Manhattan, a runaway fugitive who doesn't talk about her dark past. But I'm pretty sure being a dorky virgin would destroy my credibility.

Dad and Kira are waiting at Penn Station when I get off the train, having made it almost two hundred pages into *The Corrections*.

We all hug, and I snatch Matilda like an old witch dying to eat up pretty little babies. She has gotten bigger, much more of a heft in my arms, and she's starting to look like more of a person than a baby—more like the pretty girl she'll become. She smiles and grabs my thumb.

"Wow, you look so different!" says Kira, smiling widely. She looks perfect as usual, the kind of person who's glowing with invisible makeup and secrets about staffers at the *Paris Review*. My dad looks basically the same, just a little older and a little happier, probably because he is.

"Let me take that." He shoulders my backpack and grunts. "God, what do you have in here, bricks?"

"Your birthday present."

His eyes light up. "Oh! Did you start reading it?"

I nod.

"What do you think?"

Truthfully, it kind of annoyed me, but I don't want to let him down.

"It's amazing!" I enthuse, swallowing my real opinion. He beams, a smile like a blinking neon *That Is Correct!* sign.

Dad and Kira's place is the real estate version of a Wes Anderson movie. The Astonishing Bespoke Writerly Apartment. I throw my stuff down on the sofa, the poor-kid voice in my head immediately chastising me for making this really nice place filthy. They made up the couch for me.

There's a huge framed vintage poster of Antonioni's *Blow-Up* in the bedroom and a reclaimed-wood dining table. The apartment has high ceilings, expensive-looking light fixtures, eclectic art, and the unfamiliar house smell that I associate with rich people. Halfway through a glass of Diet Coke, I look down and notice I'm drinking out of a mason jar. Dawn and I don't even put napkins on our laps when we eat takeout.

"Before the book party, we should probably talk," says my dad, shooting a look at Kira, who nods.

"I'm gonna put her down," Kira says, carrying the baby into the other room. Matilda waves goodbye at me, her fat little hand opening and closing like a fleshy starfish. I smile a little bit, unable to help it.

"She's, like, the Tom Cruise of babies," I say.

"I know." He beams. I stop smiling.

"Did you eat?"

"Yeah," I lie.

"So I wanted to talk to you about my book."

"You don't have t—"

"I just didn't want you to go in without knowing a little bit about it."

I shake my head. "Dad, I don't need to know anything. I'm really happy for you."

"Scarlett, I really think you should listen to me. I wrote it a long time ago, and things were very different, and I don't want you to go into this without knowing some context."

I understand why he's worried—he wrote this a long time ago, when he was married to Dawn, and it's probably at least a little semiautobiographical. But I get it. Fanfic Scarlett is at once me and not me, and Gideon is him but not him, and that's hard for people to understand. I wish there was something I could say to make him feel better. The party is only a few hours from now, and he must be freaking out.

"It's gonna be great," I say. "And I do have some context, considering I was there."

Kira glides back out from the bedroom, sliding a coaster under my mason jar. I stare at her helplessly.

"Will you tell him not to be such a worrywart?"

She glances at him and says nothing, which is a little strange.

The party is at a little indie bookstore near their apartment, bursting with people and exposed brick and staff recommendations of obscure poetry I've never heard of. Jazz plays quietly in the background, like something out of a Woody Allen movie, and by the time we get there, an absurdly long and twisty line has formed around the bookshelves for the free wine a cute twentysomething girl dumps unceremoniously into Solo cups.

The minute we walk in, people are hugging my dad and coming up and congratulating him, air-kissing Kira and crooning over Matilda's pretty dress and matching bow. I am wearing the red dress I wore to the Halloween dance, and I'm getting looks that are very different from the looks Kira, Dad, and Matilda are getting. It is the difference between looking at an expensive and coveted objet d'art and looking at a slab of meat on a grill. I think I recognize some of these writers, like I've read or at least skimmed books they've written.

After I wander around the bookstore and flip through other new releases, sipping on my wine, I join the small group that has formed around Dad and Kira, where some balding guy is talking.

". . . it's almost like if you're a straight white man, you're not allowed to have an opinion anymore. When you think about it, *we're* the most oppressed group in America."

I make a face at Kira. She gives me the tiniest, imperceptible shake of her head: *Not worth it.*

I go back for a second glass of wine. Ahead of me on line, a guy with a flannel shirt solemnly tells another guy with a flannel shirt, "I've decided I'm going to try to take myself more seriously."

When I return, some older man in a suit with purple wine lips is talking my dad's ear off, and I tune in and out.

". . . wanted to talk to you about the *Observer* review because I immediately thought he didn't get the point about the epigraph. That Tolstoy quote is overused for a reason, you know? In any case, that guy doesn't know what he's talking about, and I heard that your editor at Random House gave his novel a pass, so of course he's not going to . . ."

I get on the wine line and wait for somebody to stop me. Nobody does. He must be talking about that Tolstoy quote about families, I guess: They're all fucked up in their own way, or whatever it is. Meanwhile, that guy is still braying drunkenly from across the bookstore.

". . . and you know how it is. They really rolled a lot of PR out for this title, and whenever anything is presented as the Next Great American Novel, the critics are going to want to be contrarian. So you got panned in a few major outlets! Who cares? Nobody reads the *Washington Post* anyway!"

"Sure," Dad says mildly.

"And yes, naturally some of their thoughts are valid, you know that. It's a debut. I mean, the daughter character is an issue. . . ."

Dad nods politely.

"But stay strong, buddy! I remember what this is like, and I was a kid when my first novel came out, so at least you're not a twenty-nine-year-old 'literary genius,' you know?"

Jesus, this guy.

"Hey, you want a drink? Let me get you a drink; everything's gonna be okay. Don't take it so personally."

Then he starts talking about Paramount unfairly low-balling Dad on the movie rights—which I had absolutely zero knowledge of, incidentally—and he should really switch agents. Wine in hand, I walk over to them.

"There's gonna be a movie?" I'm incredulous. "What? That's insane! How could you not tell me that?"

Dad rolls his eyes. "It's a circus."

He doesn't elaborate.

I hit up the ladies' room. When I come out of the stall to wash my hands, I find Kira trying to juggle a sleeping Matilda and simultaneously reapply her eyeliner; for once, she's not effortlessly succeeding. I walk over to her and take Matilda, a soft, warm weight in my arms. Kira looks in the mirror and says nothing, just smiles tersely at me. She places her eyeliner back into the zip pocket of her purse, I hand Matilda back to her, and she walks out of the bathroom.

At this point, maybe from the wine, I start to feel a little nauseous.

But after I leave the bathroom, I go back on the wine line again, and then again, and finally wander over to the display of signed copies of my dad's book. *The daughter character is an issue,* I think, fairly tipsy now. I pick one up, running my finger over his signature, a burst of pride washing over me.

I read the blurbs, from writers famous enough that even Dawn has probably heard of them.

A tragicomic roman à clef that may well be the modern answer to Updike's Rabbit, Run *. . . A male protagonist in the vein of Roth and Bellow . . . One man's emotionally fraught journey from an unhappy marriage and frustrated life to salvation . . .*

I turn to the epigraph:

Happy families are all alike; every unhappy family is unhappy in its own way.

I feel a spike of annoyance as I begin flipping through. He couldn't have picked a more original epigraph?

John had long ago tired of being the only adult in the house, remembering to pick up Sara from school while Kelly forgetfully guzzled a bottle of white wine and sang along to Avril Lavigne.

John watches as Kelly flirtatiously asks the twenty-two-year-old waiter his zodiac sign, then checks out his ass as he walks away.

John wonders why Sara turned out so unlike the cute, sunny teenage girls he'd had crushes on in high school.

John doesn't understand why Kelly won't talk to Sara about why she's stopped eating, the evasive jokes she makes to the many therapists they've spent thousands of

John wants to scream at them both about how selfish they

John looks at Sara's babysitter's low-cut top and can't help but notice her

John wishes he could just

John knows

John is

John feels

John feels

John f

Little dots of hurt flash white in front of my eyes. I feel smothered with jazz and the buzzing conversations and one-sided stories and stifling self-congratulation.

If John is being honest with himself, it bothers him that his daughter is the kid at school nobody likes.

I chug the rest of my Solo cup down. I lose count of the times I get back on the wine line.

Kira is kissing my dad goodbye; Matilda has stopped dozing and started getting fussy and needs to go to bed. Kira waves goodbye to me and says I'll see her at home. I think I say goodbye to her. My dad is talking to more men. I realize there are an equal amount of men and women in this room, but only the men are talking and the women are listening.

". . . daughter is about to start reading David Foster Wallace, and it makes me want to reread *Infinite Jest*." Dad gestures for me to come join the conversation he is having with three plaid-shirted, hip-bespectacled acolytes. I drink the remainder of my thousandth cup of wine, let it roll off my limp, flat palm onto a bookshelf, and walk up behind them. Almost immediately, someone from the publishing house leads Dad away to shake hands with some other people.

One of the flannels is smirking at me. I don't like the way they're looking at me. They're not leering—I'd almost prefer that. They just look smug.

"So what are you, seventeen?" asks Flannel B.

"Sixteen," I say.

"God, I can't imagine comprehending *Infinite Jest* at that age," says Flannel A, shaking his head. The other two flannels nod, and they all look slightly envious, like, *Yeah, totally, what an awesome thing to be a super-worshipped brilliant literary guy, he was so lucky other than the horrific mental illness that tortured him to death.*

"You're a writer too, I heard," Flannel B says.

"Yeah."

"Fiction?"

"Fanfiction."

Flannel A chuckles. Flannel B nudges him, like, *She's serious*.

"About what?"

"*Lycanthrope High*."

"Isn't that that werewolf show?"

I bristle.

Dad glances over, senses some kind of tension, and comes back.

"Right now she's reading *The Corrections*," Dad says and puts a proud hand on my shoulder.

"I saw Franzen speak last year. He was brilliant," says Flannel B. "How are you liking the book?"

"It's bullshit," I snap. "Are you aware that there's a line, an actual line in that book, that goes: 'At thirty-two, Denise was still beautiful'? At *thirty-two*. Denise. Was still beautiful."

There is a moment of reproachful silence with jazz under it, as if I'd just crapped on the floor and only Duke Ellington did not seem to mind.

"And it's not just Franzen! I tried to read *Infinite Jest*, but I had to stop on page 167 when Orin is screwing that single mom because he does that, because that's indicative of how interesting and tortured and fucked up he is? And it says in the paragraph—do you remember this?—that after they had sex, he traced an infinity sign on her back, and, to paraphrase, that she was so *stupid* that she thought it was an eight."

"I don't know if it says——"

"This woman is a single mom, holding down some awful job so she can feed her kid, and being judged for dating when she has the time, and just doing *the best she can* . . ." I get a little choked up. I can tell by Dad's face he just figured out why I'm upset.

"——and she sleeps with a guy who thinks he's smarter than her. And she knows that. Because she's *not* stupid, even though he thinks she is, or even if everybody thinks she is. And he traced what could be an eight *or* an infinity sign on her back after they had sex. Of course she wouldn't think it was an infinity sign. Because that would be romantic. It makes no sense that some asshole who doesn't respect you would do that. She's *not stupid*."

I'm being too loud. People are looking over at us, but I don't care. I don't want to make a scene, I'm just a little tipsy and a lot sad and I just want to ruin everything that everyone in this room holds sacred.

Flannel C, the oldest, says gently but authoritatively, "Orin's not supposed to be a nice char——"

"It's not Orin saying he thinks she's stupid, it's the God voice saying she's stupid. It's not the character, it's the *writer*. I understand the difference between omniscient narration and a close third. That's your problem, you assume everyone else is stupid, but they're not!"

Now everybody's actively staring at me. Dad smiles briskly at onlookers, trying to pull me aside.

"Scarlett, calm down." He looks pained, like he's the prom queen and I'm dumping a bucket of blood on him. He gives the Flannels a look and tries to take me aside into a quiet corner, shushing me. "This is why I wanted to talk to you—"

"Leave me alone," I yell, backing away, knocking over a pile of his display copies. A fierce burning behind my eyes threatens to spill out any second. I can't stand it in here for another minute, and I stumble out into the street without my coat, my whole body tingling all over with panic, trying to breathe through the sudden tunnel vision, feeling like I might throw up.

I am waiting for xLoupxGaroux to come get me, in a very public Starbucks where I most certainly can't get chopped into tiny pieces and hidden under his floorboards. Luckily, he was on Gchat when I logged in from my phone and put out an SOS call. It took me a while to persuade him to meet me. He kept saying he didn't think it was a good idea. But finally he relented.

"Scarface?"

I look up, shocked by the voice. An attractive, bigger, thirtysomething woman in a cute cardigan is standing over me, a preppy-ish trench coat folded over her arm.

"Umm, hi," she says.

I feel like I may have stumbled into an alternate universe.

"What?"

"You're Scarface, right?"

"Yeah."

"Real name?"

"Scarlett. You?"

"Maura." She breaks into a really lovely smile. "It's so nice to finally meet you!"

We hug.

"Wow, I am just—I don't know what I was expecting, but . . ."

Maura nods, understanding. "You assumed I was a gay man."

"Kind of. Yeah."

"There's a really large contingency of lady slash fans, y'know."

"Yeah, I do know that. Or, you know, intellectually, I was aware of that. I just . . . yeah. Looking back, nobody ever . . ."

"Asked me if I was a man or a woman? Yeah. It happens. Not that I'm making it clear myself." She shrugs and sits down.

It all makes sense now, I realize, and say, "And that's why you didn't want to meet up with me."

She sighs, stirring her coffee. "I was afraid if we met IRL, you'd be all surprised, and it would ruin everything."

"I know the feeling." I sigh.

"I hope I haven't disappointed you."

"Of course not!"

She raises her eyebrows—the exact expression I'd pictured on xLoupxGaroux whenever (s)he said "spill it" or "waiting for the truth."

"No, really. Assuming things about people makes an ass out of you and me." I stare into the swirling eye of my caramel macchiato. "Mostly me."

We chat a little bit over our coffee. Maura tells me she's a freelance graphic designer for a few major companies, but what she really wants to do is draw comics. We mourn *Lycanthrope High* for a while and finally get back to talking about ourselves IRL.

I give her the latest on Gideon and Ashley (whom Maura keeps accidentally referring to as Ashbot, sending us both into fits of giggles). I mention he was into *Lycanthrope* too and flaked on lending me some of the graphic novels.

Maura rolls her eyes.

"There'll be more. God, so many. You won't even remember him eventually."

"Are you . . . with someone? Married?"

"God no. Single, dating." Maura shrugs. "It's so early to settle down, you know? There's so much I haven't done or haven't seen. I still feel pretty young. Most of my IRL friends have had babies, and it's like . . . I feel like entire *friendships* have devolved into just . . . trying not to say that their baby is ugly."

I laugh. Relieved I'm not judging her, she laughs too.

"But I guess everything seems dull compared to the show, you know?"

"Totally."

"I want a William." She pauses, then adds, "*And* a Connor. And a video camera. I had really high expectations of New York.

I thought this was where all the freaks go! No such luck."

I laugh. "Right, I thought . . . Actually, I always thought I *knew* that I wanted to live in New York after high school. Now, I'm not so sure."

"How come?"

I lower my voice, look her dead in the eye, and ask, "Isn't everybody here kind of full of shit?"

She lets out an infectious laugh that makes the whole Starbucks shine for a minute.

"People are kind of full of shit everywhere," she concurs. "But you're a little young to be jaded already, aren't you?"

"I think it's the opposite."

"What do you mean?"

"I think I'm getting un-jaded."

Whether or not Maura understands, she lays her hand on mine.

"Well, I'm always around if you want to talk. On or off Gchat."

When we say goodbye at the subway, she asks if I'm going to tell the others on the board that we met.

"Do you want me to?"

For the first time, she looks vulnerable, like she doesn't know how to answer. Before she does, I shake my head.

"It's your story to tell."

On the one ten A.M. train back to Melville with three other passengers—two sleeping, one sketchy—I watch the city skyline recede like I usually do, but it's the first time I'm glad to leave it behind. Not that being back home is much better. I wish I could just stay on this train, a safe, in-between nowhere.

I finally check my phone. Fifteen texts from Avery. Slightly more than usual. She probably just had sex with Mike and all fifteen are "interesting" tidbits of physiological info copy-pasted from the "Sexual Intercourse (humans)" Wiki page. I don't even have the energy to tell her my life has turned into a Dr. Seuss book called *Oh the Assholes at Home and the Assholes You'll Meet*.

Before I get a chance to open any of the texts, she calls me. I answer.

"Hi. Pregnant yet?"

"Oh God, I'm so sorryyyyy," Avery wails, not sounding like herself. She repeats it over and over raggedly: "I'm sorry, I'm sorry, I'm sorry, I'm sorry, please don't be mad at me, I'm sorry."

chapter twenty

FOR THE REMAINDER of the train ride, I piece together what happened, Law & Order style: Mike came early to pick Avery up for a movie. Avery closed but didn't shut off her laptop. Ashley went into Avery's room because she wanted to e-mail herself Avery's AP History essay. Avery had been reading the last Ordinaria chapter on the Were-Heads message board.

Ashley read the chapter. She read all the chapters. Then she sent them to Gideon.

My basic nightmare, essentially. Created by Dick Wolf. *Donk-donk.*

"It's not your fault," I lie to a hyperventilating Avery, as one of the other passengers wakes up with a start and glances curiously at me. "Come on. Calm down."

"I just wasn't thinking!"

"It's really okay."

"I'm so sorry!"

"It's fine."

"Ashley's been crying in her room for like an hour."

I'm taken aback by this. *"What?"*

"You really hurt her feelings, Scarlett."

"I hurt *her* feelings?" I'm aghast.

Ashley's been hurting my feelings for the past seven years. But everything feels different now. I've been a bully too, just in a different way. I guess good writing is like an X-Man power, a magic trick, and I abused it.

"What are you gonna do?" asks Avery.

An excellent question, considering the only real choice I have is to move to the People's Republic of Totally Screwed. Gideon must be so weirded out by this, and nothing's worse than freaking out the person you like; it'd be way less embarrassing to just be hated. A burst of fear crashes in on me, as if it's coming from outside my own body, the first tidal wave of a panic attack.

"I have to go."

I hang up on her.

Dawn's car is idling in neutral in the desolate parking lot of the Melville stop when I get off the train at a little past two in the morning. As soon as she sees me, Dawn jumps out and slams the door, her North Face jacket hastily thrown over pajama pants, and starts screaming.

"Where the hell have you been?"

"Wait, stop, I—"

"Your dad and Kira have been looking for you all night! I thought you were lying dead in some bar bathroom! How could you do this?"

"I'm sorry," I mumble, echoing Avery, but about something so much bigger that two words can't begin to cover. The tears I held in in front of Dad and Kira at that awful book party finally start to fall and don't stop.

Dawn is astounded, the anger melting off her face.

"What happened? Please tell me. You're scaring me. Did somebody hurt you?"

This time she's the one working the *Gilmore Girls/Jeopardy!* technique on me, trying her best to get me to open up so she can suck the pain out of me like it's poison. But all I can do is cry harder.

"I'm sorry, Mom," I sob as she wraps me in a confused hug. "I'm sorry."

Waking up for school on Monday feels like I'm taking doomed steps up a few rickety wooden stairs to a guillotine.

I always thought part of the reason I didn't like school was that nobody knew what I was actually good at. Turns out, it's the opposite. Now that I know at least three people read my stories who are sort of *in* my stories—and, oh God, if his reading level is above picture books, Mike Neckekis makes four—what needs to happen today is that I avoid them at all costs, even if it means cutting class. Which I do. Mr. Radford's class is the first I bail on to hide in the library stacks instead.

The library remains a safe haven for approximately three minutes until I realize that Gideon is sitting at one of the computers with his arms crossed, watching me crouch behind the astrology section like a nervous rodent.

This is a nightmare.

But then I get a little indignant. *He's* the one who's been running hot and cold with me for months. *He's* the one who flirts with me in private, then ignores me in public. At least *I* told the truth. I mean, I told the truth in a speculative fiction serial on the Internet, but I told the truth. How hard could it be to tell the truth to his face?

I tentatively slink out from behind astrology, wondering if my horoscope this week was "Pisces: Your World Will Implode," and confront him.

"Hey," I say.

His expression remains ice-cold.

"'*Hey*'?" he repeats. "Really?"

"Well . . ." I scuff my sneaker against the linoleum, ashamed. "There's not really a handbook for this."

He looks lost. Angry and lost.

"I just don't really know what to say, you know?"

Actually, I don't know. He's acting like I've been calling the shots this whole time and all he's done is react to my insanity. I have a memory-flash of something Dawn said in a family-therapy session, right before my dad split—*He's calm* but wrong, and I'm loud but right, but since he's calm, it always seems like he's right.

"Did you talk to Ashley? She's really upset," he says in the same placating voice.

"Why do you like her? You're supposed to be with me," I blurt out.

His eyes widen. All the kids at the computer cubicles put on very intent fake-not-listening faces, like they are way too engrossed in copy-pasting a Wikipedia article about feudalism to pay any attention to this ridiculous live-action telenovela we're performing in the middle of the library.

"Are you kidding right now?" he asks with ice in his voice, raising his eyebrows.

"No! You've been——"

The librarian glares at me and raises a passive-aggressive two fingers. (When the faculty want us to quiet down, they have this infinitely irritating peace-sign gesture that means "quiet," occasionally supplemented by the specific and immensely irritating phrase "Heads up, hands up.")

I lower my voice incrementally. "You keep jerking me around. And I'm not just talking about the past couple of weeks. You've been trying to play both sides for a really long time, and I can't just keep sitting around waiting for you to *choose* me, Gideon."

He glances around wildly, his face bright red, as if we are in a scandalous French sex farce where he is a common waiter and I'm a married duchess who just took my boobs out.

"Why . . . dude, why are you bringing this up now?"

"This has been going on for too long," I hiss.

"I don't even know how to feel about any of this." He gestures at his computer screen, where the last chapter of the thing I wrote glares mercilessly at me. "You don't see how this is weird for me? At least I try, Scarlett. I mess up, but I try to talk to people and be open and see where they're coming from."

"By making fun of the losers and the fat kids, right? Wow. That's amazing."

"As opposed to you? You just cross your arms and judge everybody else and just—sometimes it's like you suck the air out of the room."

I look down, pushing my hand against my forehead, feeling like my brain could explode at any moment.

He lowers his voice. "How could you write that stuff about me? About my family? I just—I can't believe you'd do something like that."

He's shaking his head, horrified, like I'm Frankenstein's monster, refusing to even look at me.

"I'm sorry, I really didn't—"

"It's like you're always *testing* me or something."

"I don't mean to." My voice comes out small.

"Well, if it matters now, I, um . . . I thought I did like you. Or, I think I do. I don't know. You just make it so hard." He X-es out of the browser and stands up, grabbing his book bag and storming off.

"What makes it so hard?" I ask as he walks away.

He comes striding back and gets really, really close to me

and says, "You can't have an inferiority complex *and* a superiority complex. Just pick one."

Then he does actually storm off.

I feel the tingling in my arms and legs that I know means the beginning of a panic attack, and I barrel into the girls' bathroom by the band hallway. I brace myself against the sink and stare into the mirror, trying to tell the anxious girl reflected back at me that everything's going to be fine. The more I freak, the weirder I'll act, and the worse it'll be.

I'm reaching for the emergency Xanax I keep rolled in a plastic bag in my pencil box when I hear a sniffle from the handicapped stall. I glance over and see a plume of smoke drifting from above the chipped iron walls. I clear my throat.

A familiar, tearful whine: "Who's out there?"

"Ashley? Is that you?"

Silence.

"Go away, you bitch," she snaps, choking up. I walk over and stand outside the stall, leaning my ear toward the door. I hear the little crinkly burns from the end of the cigarette as she inhales deeply.

"I wanna talk to you. Come on, let me in."

"No."

"Listen. I really didn't mean for anybody to read that thing."

"What!" she gasps, then starts sort of laugh-crying. "You didn't write it in your little freak diary under your bed. You put it on the *Internet*."

"Yeah, I did, it's this website for——stories you can write for people to read, and I have some friends on that site, and it's just, like, something I do for fun. Please just let me in. I'm really sorry."

I hear a rusty click, and she kicks the stall door open with her Frye boot, leaving her leg stretched out so it's hard for me to come in. A neat pile of menthol butts are lined up in a row on top of the toilet paper dispenser.

Her eyes are puffy and red. She looks right up at me. "Why do you think I'm so dumb? And don't lie. I'll know."

"Because you're mean to me."

Perplexed, she wrinkles her nose, like I've put a rip in the space-time continuum. "You're mean to *me*."

"What? I've never said one mean thing to you."

She holds out the pack of Camels, offering me one with sort of a challenging attitude. I take one, grab the lighter from the top of the toilet bowl, and inhale as she watches me closely. My eyes water, but I refuse to cough.

"You don't hold it in like weed. Just exhale," she says, smirking.

I do, making my chest burn like hell, and then I double over coughing.

"I wasn't dancing on that divider," I croak.

She rolls her eyes. "What are you even talking about?"

"You know what I'm talking about. How you always call me 'Divider' and treat me like nothing because I'm poor and my mom is single and cleans your house. And for some reason, for the past seven years, you have thought all that's totally hilarious."

"Um, yeah," she sniffles, "because you think I'm a fucking moron."

"I—"

"And you convinced Avery I am too. She's my sister! When you're not around, we're really close. But whenever you're there, she acts different. You have your smart, special club, and I'm just a dumb Fembot idiot. Right?" She wipes her eyes with the back of her hand, smearing her gold shadow.

"Even my parents like you more than me, even though I get straight As and your grades suck. They always talk about how shitty your mom is and how you deserve better, and what a smart, great kid you are. You come over for dinner, and they talk to you about books and stuff more than they ever talk to me about *anything*. And *he* likes you more too."

"Who?"

She lolls her head and gives me this *Oh, don't bullshit me* look.

"You mean Gideon?"

"Duh, I mean Gideon. He's liked you the whole time. Probably because you're pretty and skinny and have big boobs, and you know it. I'm not a boy; I can see right through your crap. You pretend you don't know or care, and you wear weird glasses and Chucks and you'll watch his stupid old stand-up specials with him, so he thinks you're cooler or smarter than me or some dumb shit like that." She sniffs fiercely.

"You took my sister away from me, so I wanted to take him away from you. And I thought maybe it would give you a reality check, so you'd stop being delusional about some exclusive club you're in just for being a snobby asshole to everybody. That's how it started."

But not how it ended. That's when I realize it from behind her words: He hurt her just like he hurt me. She stubs out her butt angrily and tosses it in the toilet bowl.

"But now he hates you. And I didn't even have to do that; you did it yourself."

She pushes past me, the stall door slamming closed, and stops by the mirrors. Through a sliver in the joints of the stall walls, I can see her fixing her hair and dabbing the smeared makeup off her cheekbones.

I feel like someone just put hot wax all over who I am, laid a strip down over it, and then ripped everything right off, and now there's nothing left.

Dazed, my eyes wander to the wall and land on *Scarlett Epstein is a slut*, still there from when I scrawled it in Sharpie two years ago as a joke that now seems snide and terminally unfunny. I mindlessly fix my eyes on it until the words lose their meaning.

Ashley pulls her hair into a severe, careless ponytail, with those little lumps sticking out that girls with straight hair always get.

"I'm sorry," I say.

"No, you're not. Honestly, it's not a big deal. Keep pretending I'm the dumb, mean, hot girl and you're some weird, ugly outcast nobody likes, if you really need to feel like you're better than me."

I hear the door of the girls' room open and shut, and she's gone.

I breathe again, sort of, but quick and short, like a fragile reptile in the wrong climate. I slide down the wall. I can barely feel it when I hit the floor.

chapter twenty-one

He thrust into her a bunch of times. "I love you," he whispered into her ear. She moaned because it felt so good, and replied breathlessly: "I suck."

I suck. "*A bunch of times*"? Even if that's technically how sexual intercourse works, you'd think I could do a little better than that. The forum is pretty desperate for a sex scene, so I'm trying to give them what they want, but it isn't happening. Normally I don't even have to delete a sentence and try again. To be honest, I don't feel like writing—I haven't for a while now, actually— but they're kind of my only friends besides Ruth and Avery now. Both of whom have called a few times, but I put a kibosh on my phone after my dad left a few apologetic messages. I don't feel ready to pick up and talk to anybody just yet.

Okay, let's go.

He thrust into her hard, but not so hard that it seemed like he had an anger problem or anything, just the normal amount of hard. It felt good. It felt great, actually!

He thrust into her a few times, and it felt like how that feels for people who have had sex.

He thrust(ed?)

Forget "thrust"; it's gross. And "into her" used to confuse me in the fourth grade when I was sneaking Dawn's Jodi Picoult novels, because it kind of seems like a weird metaphor. Right? "He is inside her" doesn't sound literal; it sounds like some kind of strange aphorism for "He lives inside of her heart, forever" or something.

He climbed on top of her and moved around, like one does.

Maybe I'm not good at writing anymore. Wouldn't that be funny? Yes and no!

"That feels really great," she said.
"I'm so glad, thanks," he said.
"No, thank you," she said.
"You're welcome?"

Wait, why am I—why is she, I mean—thanking him? He's not helping her build an IKEA cabinet. You don't thank people for having sex with you, I don't think, unless maybe you're disfigured or seven hundred years old or something.

"This feels really good!" she said.
"For me, also!"

Ughhhhhhhhhhhhhhhhhh, this is bad.
Delete all.

I trudge toward Ruth's house with a copy of my dad's book. I'm giving her mine—something tells me it deserves about as much valuable real estate on the bookshelf in my room as Nicole "Snooki" Polizzi's *A Shore Thing*. I wonder what she'll say about it. Probably something like, "The literary world needs another white male perspective like I need these shingles on my ass," or some other perfect withering quip.

I knock on her door, and nobody answers. I glance back at the garden, checking to see if she's crouched in the sunflower patch, lighting up. She's not. I knock again harder, and the door creaks open by itself.

"Ruth?" I yell, tentatively stepping inside. "Are you home?"

I walk through the foyer, following that never-ending shelf of feminist literature that winds all the way into the bedroom. I've never been in there before; our relationship has always been contained to the garden, the porch, the foyer, and the kitchen. (And, on one memorable occasion, the bathroom. I walked in on her puking. "Schnapps," she explained as she choked over the toilet, before I ran to get her a glass of water.)

After hesitating for a second, I push the door open.

The bedroom is small with one bright window, illuminating tiny dust particles that float across the room. Posters of classic French films from the sixties hang on the wall, their yellowed edges curling up and inward. A ceramic ashtray shaped like a mermaid sits directly on the mattress, filled with cashed joints and the black dregs of weed.

That's when I see the pill bottles—thirty at least, neatly stacked on a mirrored tray next to the bed with the exception of one bottle, which lies on its side, empty. On the nightstand, draped over a water-damaged copy of *The Handmaid's Tale*, an oxygen mask lies coiled like a snake.

"Ruth?" My voice comes out a squeak, then I find it again. "Ruth!"

The house is empty, but she's still everywhere. She must be out grocery shopping, or buying fertilizer, but even as I'm telling myself this, I know. I just know, somehow, and I have no idea how I could've been so clueless this entire time.

I bolt out of the house, hearing the screen door slam and bounce a few times behind me, and vault over the flowers. I think this is what disassociation is—seeing through a shaky camera, hearing your own heavy breathing like a heroine in a horror movie. I hurtle up the apartment stairs two at a time.

"Dawn!"

She appears from around the corner in her uniform, wrapping

up her hair under the headband she uses when she cleans.

"Is everything okay?" she asks, alarmed.

"It's Ruth, she's not home, she's always home at this time, and I went in—" I double over gasping, sinking with dread like an anchor. "We need to call the hospital. Something's really wrong, the door was unlocked, and—I think I'm gonna faint."

"Sit down and breathe. Okay? Are you listening? We're gonna figure this out."

Intellectually, I want to brush her aside and call every hospital in Central Jersey immediately. But the dizziness overtakes me, blurring my vision and forcing me to plop down on the floor. Dawn grabs her cell phone.

She speaks brusquely to someone on the phone for an indeterminate amount of time, then calls someone else and speaks to them too. The whole time I try to breathe, to stay calm.

Dawn turns to me, holding her iPhone slightly away from her, and says, "They took her to Robert Wood Johnson. I'm calling them now."

I stumble to my feet and lurch for the door, still seeing everything through a weird fish-eye lens of panic, my own hand looking odd as it reaches for the knob. Dawn holds out her hand to stop me and listens to the voice on the other end.

"Yes, she came in—no, we're not blood relatives, but my daughter is very—I see," Dawn murmurs, her face almost immediately becoming a subdued mask so that I know exactly what she's going to tell me when she hangs up the phone. It'll be any minute now, and that will make it real. All I can really do is wait and hope I'm wrong. Dawn scribbles down another number on the back of an unopened bill, hangs up, and calls that one. After I don't know how long, maybe ten minutes, she finally hangs up.

"Scarlett, she's gone."

"Like . . . what do you mean?"

"They took her to the hospital last night. She wasn't alone; she had a friend with her named Sally. Do you know her?"

I shake my head, beyond guilty. I didn't even know Ruth had any other friends.

"I just spoke to her. She told me Ruth had been very sick for a very long time."

"I mean, she was really old, but she seemed totally—"

"She had breast cancer for years. When it came back this time, it was terminal, and she decided to stop treatment. She passed away early this morning."

I feel myself just stupidly shaking my head.

"Why would she do that?" I whisper.

"I didn't ask."

"She called me a bunch of times the other night. I didn't pick up." I pull up her name on my cell phone's missed-call list. "See? Look!"

There she is, RUTH, at seven thirty-two P.M., eight oh three P.M., and nine twenty P.M. For some reason, that is when I actually feel it, the fact of it undeniably hitting every part of me at once, like an ice-bucket challenge. *Ruth is dead*, just punching me in the stomach and casually walking away.

"Oh my God. I had no idea," I hear myself say. "Oh my God. How did I not see it?"

"Scar, listen, baby. Can you just listen? Scarlett."

I can't, though. I let myself tumble back down on the floor and start to cry, these weird gulpy shock-tears, like how kids cry right after they fall down.

"From the way her friend made it sound, Ruth was in control, and she decided how she wanted it to go."

Her words remind me of the way parents tell their kids about a dog they just put down. *She was really old, so we brought her to a farm where she can run and play.* It doesn't make up for anything that really happened; it's just a nicer way to frame the truth.

"There was nothing anybody could have done," Dawn says, trying to reassure me, but it just makes me feel worse, because Ruth was dying and I wasted so much of her time talking about a stupid boy.

I surprise myself by becoming furious with Ruth—a fury that almost feels like an anxiety attack. If she'd deigned to talk to a doctor for a single hour out of the zillions of hours I talked her ear off about Gideon, she might still be alive. For all the time she wasted with me, shooting the shit and smoking weed, she couldn't go to the hospital for forty minutes and thoroughly discuss her options? The rational part of my brain knows I have no right to be angry at her, and I should even be proud of her, but I'm so mad that she didn't tell me.

She just slipped off with no one the wiser, all noble and dignified. What a bullshit move.

chapter twenty-two

I'VE CRIED AND CRIED, but I don't feel like I've even gotten below the surface of it. It's like I'm skating on a frozen lake, with no idea how deep the water underneath the ice goes, or how cold it is, waiting for it to crack and for me to plunge in. I don't have the energy to talk to anybody or to write. The only thing I've done in the past few days is look up the Kübler-Ross model and discover, to my disappointment, that Kübler-Ross is one person, whereas I'd always pictured that Kübler and Ross were two lifelong best friends until Kübler passed away in a freak umlaut accident and Ross was left bereft on his knees, screaming, "KÜBLERRRRR!" And eventually he got it together and put his grief to good use by coming up with those stages.

Apparently when you show up to school for a week straight wearing pajamas and your unwashed hair in a topknot that bats might fly out of any moment, people get concerned. At some point, I spent one of these free-floating chunks of disoriented time in the hot seat in Mr. Barnhill's perpetually burned-coffee-smelling office, where they plop down the cutters and potential bomb threat–makers to get to the bottom of how serious it is. Like you're in a film noir movie with one swinging overhead light, except instead of the murder of an aspiring showgirl who got mixed up with Peter Lorre, it's feelings.

". . . learned recently that you've had a loss," Mr. Barnhill is saying. Of hearing, I wish. But I nod a little, the minimum required for him not to send me to the principal's office for lack of participation.

"How are you feeling?"

He appears to be wondering what the most sensitive way to approach death with a student while eating a cruller might be.

"Fine," I hear myself reply.

He bites into the cruller, pauses, then gingerly puts it back down on a napkin.

"There have been concerns from some of your teachers— when they ask you questions, you don't hear them. That you seem to be preoccupied lately."

Not one class here has ever occupied me, I think.

"In any case." Mr. Barnhill rises and brushes some cruller crumbs off his oxford shirt. "There's some literature that I'd like you to glance over."

Mr. Barnhill sidles over to the table near the sofa where the cutters usually wait to speak with him and pulls four pamphlets out of clear plastic displays, stacking them in a pile. He hands them to me. The one on the top has a glossy photo of a sad eleven-year-old boy on the front flap and reads, "The Grieving Child in the Classroom." Underneath those, I can only assume, are the STD pamphlets students usually walk out with.

But even after that, he keeps looking at me for a long time. I realize, to my surprise, he is truly concerned. He might be a good guidance counselor; I just haven't noticed until now. Or maybe I don't have the energy to keep feeling like everyone's lame, and the curtain I've always looked through has fallen down.

"Look, I know these are really cheesy," he says. "But they can be helpful if you've never had a death in the family."

I tried that, I want to say, but speaking doesn't seem worth the effort.

I haven't been able to sleep a lot, and last night at three A.M., I hopped on my computer, Googled a lot of articles about grief, and skimmed the first couple of pages blankly. Then I clicked farther down in the results. Nothing seemed specific enough— and, I realized, nothing will. There is no Dear Sugar on how to deal with the fact that your dad would sell you into human trafficking for a *New Yorker* byline, or how to recover from the long, painful death of the nonrelated seventy-three-year-old retired lesbian feminist professor across the street who made you buy her weed.

And, even worse, somewhere around page twenty-two of the Google search results for grief advice, I began to suspect that no matter where I go after high school, my problems will never be "relatable" page-one Google-search problems. That they will in fact continue to narrow down to a tiny, sparkling pinprick that nobody can see but me.

Ruth at least should have stuck around to see her garden grow back in.

I keep thinking of it that way, like: *She should've hung out a little longer* or *She shouldn't have bailed because.* I know rationally that it wasn't her choice—that after years of fighting, she was lying in a hospital bed with her body failing even though her mind still wasn't ready—but it's easier to think of it like she got a little too high and slipped out of a party early without saying goodbye to anybody.

I've been sitting on her porch for a few hours now, gazing out at the bright paved street, half hoping that at any second the screen door will slam and she'll come out in suspenders and a white oxford, talking smack about the sex life of a woman who cut her off on the Superfresh line. I never got to tell her how much she meant to me. But even if I had the chance, I wouldn't know how to explain it. It was too long and too complicated. I would have just made jokes until she gave me a knowing, chastising look that said I was hiding behind cleverness.

"Hello. Are you Scarlett?"

I glance up to find a woman in her seventies standing over me, wearing a modest floral dress and fleece, her hair henna red.

"Hi. Yeah." I stand and shake her hand.

"I'm Sally. Ruth's friend. I spoke with your mom on the phone when she—"

"I remember."

I want to ask Sally whether she tried to change Ruth's mind when she made the choice to stop treatment. Although once Ruth was set on something, the idea of anyone trying to change it was laughable.

"I'm out here from California, just for a few weeks. I'm making the arrangements."

"I see."

Then she looks at me curiously.

"I've heard a lot about you."

"You have?"

She nods and smiles at me. "Yep. She told me you helped out in the garden."

"Yeah."

"And how you remind her of herself at your age. She said it sometimes seemed like your mom wasn't, ah"—she clears her throat—"wasn't there a lot, and Ruth tried to be there for you when she wasn't. You were very important to her, you know."

This all should make me feel good, but instead it makes the bottom drop out under my heart.

"She was ready to go, you know. More than ready. I tried to talk her out of it, but she wouldn't have it." Sally sighed. "Even toward the end, before I flew out here, she seemed very happy. She said she was finally getting to read because she wasn't nauseated all the time, and nobody treated her like a sick person."

"Mm-hmm," I say, gazing off into the middle distance, trying not to cry. I understand, now, that over-the-top Sicilian funeral in *The Godfather* where the wife is trailing after the casket, wailing. When someone close to you dies, every emotion becomes very close to the surface. The other day at school, the vending machine ate my $1.25 when I tried to buy Combos, and I almost curled into a damp, sobbing fetal position in the hallway.

Sally goes on, "I was wondering if you'd like to speak at the memorial service."

The prospect of this snaps me out of my semi-catatonia. I want to tell her that Ruth's death doesn't make me want to write, the same way my parents' divorce or my dad's idiotic novel doesn't make me want to write. It just feels too big, too fundamental to who I am now, not just something happening around me that I can perceive and filter. Let alone talk about in front of people.

I don't think I feel feelings right. I think my body processes important feelings the way people with acid reflux digest food wrong—there are abnormal holes in me that make it leak out in unexpected places here and there, and by the time it gets to the end, nothing is left to be flushed out. I don't know if I can talk about it in front of people.

"I'm not sure that I'm the right, um . . ."

"I figured you might say that. But it helps. I didn't want to speak at my husband's service, but Ruth talked me into it. She was very close with him, and she said it's what he would have wanted. And in retrospect, I'm glad I did."

I get a sudden flash of clarity, recalling the story Ruth told me about her life. "You're the widow. I mean, she told me about you."

Sally gives me a little, polite "nice to meet you" smile, as much as one can under these circumstances. "In any case, when Ruth was in the hospital, we discussed this, in so many words. And she said there wasn't anybody who could do a better job than you."

Goddamn it, Ruth. You left me like you found me: being pushed out of my comfort zone.

At least John St. Clair comes through, as usual. Or at least he did a couple of seasons ago, without knowing it. The season two finale featured an evil "boss" that Gillian had to fight—the demon turned out to be a physical manifestation of the grief she hadn't dealt with when her mentor at her old school, Mrs. Waterbury, was killed by William (when he was evil, obviously). I liked the episode then, but it turns out it's shockingly gratifying to watch when you're actually grieving, because there it is: big and mean and corporeal. Were-Heads and critics pretty much agree that it is one of the most well-done—and crushingly sad—episodes of the series.

When I get home from school, I take a long, life-affirming shower for the first time in five days. I'm sitting on the sofa in a towel, halfway through my twenty-first viewing of the episode, when someone knocks on the door. It is not a good time. The episode is almost over, and the way Gillian vanquishes the demon is by hugging it, and that scene has been making me cry for the last ten viewings.

Nevertheless, I pause the episode, jump up, and go to the door to squint out the peephole. Gideon is standing outside, shifting uncomfortably, holding a six-pack of beer.

I sigh. He knocks again, and finally I open the door.

"Oh. Um, hey," he says.

"Hi."

"Are you . . . how are you?"

"Fine," I say flatly, then I cough and say in a joking sexy voice, "Faaaaah-ne."

He smiles a little as his eyes flick up and down my small towel, followed by sort of a guilty-for-checking-me-out sigh.

"I heard about Ruth."

"Yeah."

"I'm really sorry." Then he winces. "God. Is that what you say? It just sounds so dumb. You say that when you, like, bump into people."

"It's okay. There's not really anything right to say, I think."

"I thought I'd come see if you were okay and everything."

"Thanks, I'm f—"

"Are you okay though, really? You seem not okay," he asks, stepping on my words.

"Yes. No. I don't know. Come in."

He steps inside past me, and I gesture for him to sit down on the sofa, where the episode's been paused.

"This is a sad one," he says. I guess he can recognize it from the still.

"Yeah."

"Maybe you shouldn't be watching this?" he suggests tentatively.

"Maybe. Hey, wait here, I'm gonna put some clothes on real quick. I'll be right back."

"Okay."

I run to my room and throw on the first clean clothes I can grab—a tank top and pink running shorts—and then I come back and sit on the sofa again.

"So your, like . . . story thing," Gideon says. I squirm with humiliation. "It was weird for me. I'm not gonna lie. But I know it's what you like to do. Or how you deal with things or whatever."

"I think I'm done with it." I sigh.

"With what? With writing?" he asks, surprised.

I nod and snag two beers from the six-pack. I snatch up the rest and head for the kitchen to toss them in the fridge.

"But you're so good at it!" he shouts from the living room.

"I don't know," I yell back, because I don't know. The wanting to write has to come before the writing itself, and I just haven't wanted to, which makes me think I will never want to again.

"So, I thought you might like a stand-up routine I downloaded a while ago," he yells. "It's this comedian named Tig Notaro."

Mildly surprised and secretly pleased, I yell back, "You still listen to stand-up?"

I return to the sofa with the bottle-opener magnet from our fridge and pop open both beers.

"Of course," he says, sounding surprised that I'd ask.

I hand him one.

"I don't know. I guess I thought you'd moved on to wittier influencers like Jason Tous."

He stares straight ahead, looking contrite. But he just has nothing to say for himself. I admit, I'm partly sticking it to him because at some point, it was two roads diverged in a wood: He's (rightly) upset that I wrote creepy Internet fiction about him, and I am (rightly) upset that he has transformed into a proper popular asshole. But ultimately, I don't care about any of that right now. Everything that seemed like a big deal last week is in my emotional rearview mirror.

"Well, it's nice of you to try. But I don't think I'm into any 'what's the deal with' stuff right now." I hand him a beer.

He shakes his head. "It's not that, like, not at all. I have it here on my phone. Why don't you just give it a chance? I bet you've watched this enough times you've memorized the dialogue by now." He gestures to the TV.

Fair point. I shrug.

"Sure, whatever. But I have veto power. If I'm not into it in five minutes, it's done."

"Deal."

He scrolls quickly through his iTunes library—which I quickly note consists almost entirely of Kanye and stand-up specials—at least his taste is still good—and hits play on one.

The emcee introduces the woman, Tig Notaro. I am already rolling my eyes at Gideon's tone-deaf attempt to make me feel better.

"Just wait," Gideon murmurs. My heart does a weird sputter because he looks exactly the way he used to when he was about to play me a comedian's boundary-breaking set—his eyes are shining with adrenaline, and he's leaning forward with his hands on his knees like he's about to begin a race.

As the opening applause calms down, Tig Notaro begins her set with, "Hello. I have cancer. Hello. How are you guys?" She is met with some confused giggles but mostly silence. Like the audience, I am officially listening.

For the next thirty minutes, everything fades away as she talks. She'd been diagnosed with bilateral breast cancer only three days earlier, she says, and as a professional comedian, she can't make it into neat jokes yet.

Instead, she does something amazing: She's bracingly honest. She talks about how friends felt bad, now, when they complained about petty problems in their own lives, but she genuinely wishes they would just talk to her normally. She makes fun of platitudes like "God doesn't give you anything you can't handle." She doesn't hide her fear of the future. She faces down an L.A. audience who came to hear some hip, ironic observational comedy and tells them—without packaging it into a joke-punchline format— that she just found out she might die soon. Every laugh she gets throughout the whole set is the result of her being totally, completely, un-comedian-esquely straightforward and honest.

The applause is long and thunderous and gives me enough time to realize that I'm crying. This is how Ruth must have felt when she found out, why she didn't tell anybody, how hard it is to negotiate with yourself, let alone other people. How you decide to just let go. I'm not mad at her anymore. This crying is a different kind of crying than I've been doing for the past few weeks. The ice finally broke, and now I'm underwater.

Gideon leans to the side on the sofa and wraps me in a big hug, my tears soaking into his Maclaine-house-smelling MHS hoodie, leaving a blotchy wet spot behind. This goes on for a while, but I can't tell how long. This kind of crying is a little bit like falling into a black hole: Maybe it lasts two minutes, maybe two hours, maybe you get torn apart, maybe you time travel back to 1887—you can speculate, but you can never really know.

Finally, I pull away from him, even though it feels unnatural to separate again, and I try to pull myself together. I sniffle, draw the back of my hand across my wet eyes. I wish I could yell at him for being such a jerk lately, but I'm too drained. And besides, it's too late. I already saw the glimmer in this "hot popular guy" of that chubby comedy nerd I was best friends with when we were thirteen, the weirdo who knows exactly what half-hour stand-up set will reach me through my thick armor of bullshit. Gideon is still Gideon. Maybe that's all I need to know.

A few trips back and forth to the fridge later—becoming increasingly, acutely aware (in a good way) of Gideon checking

out my butt in the neon shorts each time I go into the kitchen—
we have torn through the six-pack. I'm tipsy and laughing and feel
like the big things, the real things, are far away. I'm in a mental
place that's pretty rare for me, which is: I just want things to be
easy. Context-free. I want to be like any nondescript boy and girl
sitting on a sofa drinking beer, across America, right now.

After three beers, I drop my final bottle in "the recycling,"
a repurposed Target bag hung on the living room door, and
saunter back to the sofa.

"Hey, where's your mom?" asks Gideon. "I want to say hi."

I know exactly where she is—she's meeting Brian's mother
at that Mediterranean place downtown—but instead of going
into it, I opt for, "Out?"

"Oh, right, Out. I like that place."

I smile, even though it is an incredibly silly joke that isn't
worthy of him.

"Great tapas bar, Out," I say.

"I'm into their wine list."

"They're always so crowded, though."

"To tell you the truth, it always seemed a little overrated,"
he replies, looking at me a moment too long as he swigs his beer,
his big hand wrapped around the neck of the bottle. It's a weird
way to hold a beer. I feel a rush of affection toward him, mixed
with a mystery ingredient.

It's lust, *you idiot,* my body informs my brain. *You still like
him and like-like him, despite all his shitty transgressions as a Popular.
You liked him first, and now other people like him too, and when that*

happened, you felt like you had to stop. Scarlett Joan Epstein, you are a hipster.

He's just sitting there, leaning back against the sofa, finishing his beer, one arm sprawled over the back of the couch, so guy-ish and appealing. He catches me looking at him, and we regard each other with a mix of bemused *Are we gonna do this?* and *Is this gonna fuck everything up forever?*

In the end, he is the one who goes for it, circling my waist with both his hands. I instinctively arch my back, accessing, for the first time ever, something my body knows how to do but my brain doesn't. His warm tongue is sort of beery, but not in a bad way. We kiss for a really long time, until it starts getting more breathless and I finally straddle him, wrapping my hands around his neck as he keeps holding my waist. We seem to be taking turns craning our necks in this make-out session (which bodes well if the thing Dawn once told me is true, that whoever likes the other person more is the one who cranes their neck). Gravity begins to take over, so I start awkwardly falling backward, but his hands are so solidly wrapped around my back that I'm not scared, and he moves gently down off the sofa with me in his arms.

To my distant surprise—distant because my brain is waving goodbye as my body speeds off down the highway—we are now on the floor, me on my back, him on top of me sliding his hands down my back to grab my ass. My brain argues feebly: *But I'm so mad at him!* I gasp loudly without meaning to as he breaks away to move down and kiss my neck. My legs have wrapped around his back of their own accord, another testament to the power of biology. He slips one hand under my shirt and the other one goes for the drawstring on my shorts.

I realize this is how mistakes happen——not thinking, just doing. (Have you ever heard that Katy Perry lyric "No regrets, just love" and wondered how many teen pregnancies it inspired? I have!)

"Wait, wait, wait, wait," I breathe.

"What?" He yanks on the drawstring but accidentally knots it too tight to open, so he just tries to wedge his hand inside my shorts.

I am about to lose my virginity to an asshole just because we hung out when we were kids, says my brain.

Oh my God, please shut up, you get to drive allllllll the time, give me the keys for once, my body replies.

But my brain won't shut up. *I am about to lose my virginity to a guy who makes fun of fat people.*

"Wait, stop."

He takes his hands off me and lies on the floor, facing up and breathing shallowly. I stay on my back, also staring up at the ceiling.

"I, um, I can't."

I'm trying to sound nonplussed, like I have almost-sex with guys all the time and coolly stop short because I am playing hard to get.

"No worries! Like, not at all," Gideon says, now sounding vaguely panicked. "I——I mean, did I go too fast? Or did I do something you didn't want me to do?"

I look at him with my eyebrows raised incredulously.

"Just now? No. But the last couple of months *all* you've done is stuff I didn't want you to do."

I sit up stick-straight like I'm in an executive office chair—as if this somehow gives me more authority—trying to catch my breath.

"I mean, first of all, what about Ashley?" I ask.

He holds up his hands in an exaggerated gesture, then flops them dejectedly back down on the carpet in a very teenage-boy-didn't-get-to-have-sex way. I hope on top of hope that he has an answer both my body and my brain are down with. *Not* an answer like the one he gives me, which is: "What about her?"

The off-the-charts "guy"-ishness of that response nearly sends me sailing over the edge of my sanity.

"Are you guys dating?"

"We're just hanging out."

I groan. "Gideon, that is the dumbest euphemism in the world. It's not 'hanging out' if someone gets an IUD."

"Well, we haven't had any sort of official conversation about it! I don't know! Why are you yelling at me?"

"Because you were a dick to her!"

"Really? Since when do you care about Ashley's feelings?"

"Since I realized she had them!" I roll my head away from him, fixing on a dusty quarter underneath the sofa, feeling my eyes start to burn. "I got mad at her when I should have gotten mad at you. But at least I'm *trying* to be better," I say. "You're not even admitting you were a dick."

He sighs. "I feel bad about Ashley."

"Good. You should. But what about the other stuff? Like laughing at Leslie in class, or making fun of Jessicarose Fallon when she ran a fourteen-minute mile in gym."

He winces and claps his hand over his eyes. "I know. I've gone along with some of that stuff, even when I don't . . ."

"Are you trying to earn my sympathy? Because you won't. Just because you come over here and listen to comedy with me and act like your old self when we're alone together doesn't make everything okay."

He sits up too, looking like a dog I just kicked, and says, "I'm just trying to explain—"

"Oh, I understand completely! Whoever you're hanging out with determines which member of the Breakfast Club you're gonna be."

Getting worked up now, Gideon begins to raise his voice. "That's because I don't feel like I fit in anywhere!"

"You're just saying that because you think that's who I want you to be!" I snap back. "You think I want Judd Nelson, so you're being Judd Nelson. But at school tomorrow, when Ashley wants you to be Emilio Estevez, you'll be Emilio Estevez."

"I will *not* be Emilio Estevez!" he shouts indignantly, which would be hilarious out of context if we weren't both so angry.

"And you know the most messed-up thing? I don't even think it's an act anymore. I bet if you were alone in a room, you'd have no idea who you are. You're just, like"—I shrug, defeated—"you're a sheep. And I hate sheep."

He sits there, wounded and angry. Ever since Ruth died, I've had a pattern where, for just a few minutes, I can care intensely about some dumb thing I used to care about, but then it flickers out.

"Can you just go away?" I whisper. "Please?"

After a few seconds of silence, the floorboard creaks as he stands, gathering his stuff. He leaves without saying goodbye.

chapter twenty-three

GRIEF IS A WEIRD, quiet thing. Maybe it isn't for everybody. When Shana Miller had an aneurysm in the shower and died sophomore year, girls clustered together in the cafeteria, crying—but I don't really feel the energy to express anything, even if I felt anything, if that makes sense.

I'm at whichever stage makes me do things like stand in front of my open locker staring at nothing for three minutes, forgetting where I am or what I need to be doing.

"Scarlett?"

Mrs. Johnston, the wiry, gray-haired gym teacher who occasionally tosses off creepy asides about the absurdity of not allowing school prayer, is approaching. Before I can back away, she pulls me into a hug. It is the hug of a woman who should really have an "ample bosom" but doesn't. She almost impales me on her collarbone.

"The Lord is an everlasting rock, sweetheart."

"Aite."

"Mr. Barnhill mentioned you've just experienced a loss, and I just wanted to say that I'm here if you need anything." She speaks with gravity, like she's giving out a life achievement award at the Oscars or something. The most we have ever spoken before this is when she challenged me on the frequency of my period during the semester we had to take swim.

"Um, thank you," I say, attempting to use the same tone. Sometime this week, I figured out that the secret to being nice to everybody all the time is to just assume that everybody you interact with is going to be killed in a car crash the next day, and this is one of their final interactions on Earth. That's, like, the only way you can be nice 24/7. It somehow makes Mrs. Johnston more relatable to know she's nice because she's fantasizing about my broken body being pried from the wreckage with the Jaws of Life.

"I brought your mom a quiche."

"Yeah, thanks."

"You know"—she lowers her voice conspiratorially—"He has a plan."

"Mr. Barnhill?"

"The Lord, our God. With Jesus at his right hand."

"I'm Jewish mostly," I mumble, then say, "I have to go to the bathroom."

I head for the handicapped stall in the bathroom by the band hallway, which has become my natural habitat, a Melville tradition for emotionally bereft girls. Let's just say if Moaning Myrtle ever wants a change of scenery and doesn't mind the smell of cigarettes followed by a few sprays of Gap Dream, I know just the place.

Back home, from the solace of my bed, I hear Dawn open the front door and greet somebody, saying, "She's in her room," even though I don't feel like hanging out with anyone. I burrow back under the covers, hoping whoever it is will just go away.

"Hi."

I peek over the blanket. Avery's standing in the doorway.

"You weren't answering my texts."

I shrug. She pulls her TOMS off, one by one, hesitates for a second, then climbs into bed with me, still far enough on the edge that she's sort of hanging off. This is quite abnormal for us. Snuggling is definitely not part of our "two brains in a jar" dynamic.

"So . . . yeah, this is happening," she says, like she just heard my thoughts. I nod.

"It's kind of okay."

"Yeah."

We lie there for a minute saying nothing.

"How are you doing?"

"Fine."

She rolls her eyes, flops her arm to the bed in frustration. "Jesus, Scarlett, come on."

"I don't know. I'm . . . sad, I guess." As soon as I utter the word *sad* out loud, I make it real, which makes me tear up again. There's no end to the crying, maybe. Avery turns over to face me and moves more toward the center of the bed, close enough to me so that I can see tiny green waves in her hazel eyes.

"It's really sad," she says, plainly.

"I was just so caught up in other stuff that I didn't even . . . like, in movies, people get to say their thing to the person."

"Thing, like, what thing?"

"Their thing. Like, 'You're important to me, even though I took you for granted sometimes, and I'll miss you for *X* and *Y* reasons'—all that shit." I do air quotes. "'Closure' or whatever."

"I think that mostly only happens in movies," she says.

I nod.

"Bad movies," she says.

"I guess."

She sighs. "Scar, that's what a eulogy is. It's all the stuff you didn't think to say."

I grunt, annoyed, and turn my head toward the wall. "So Dawn told you about that?"

"Yeah, and I think you need to do it. If you don't, you'll never get to say your thing."

"Maybe." I'm being stubborn, but it still just seems like a horrible idea, going up there and freezing like a deer in headlights. "Let's just change the subject, okay?"

"Sure."

"How's Ashley?"

Ave's answer is slightly guarded. "Fine." Then she adds, almost despite herself, "She's in her room most of the time. Crying, I think."

I wonder if I look like the mean girl from where Ave's sitting, too.

She continues. "Gideon and Ashley definitely stopped doing whatever it was that they were doing. Hooking up on the regs or whatever. If that makes you feel better . . ."

"It doesn't," I say.

I'm about to confide in her what happened when Gideon came over, but something stops me. For one thing, it feels like it was ages ago now, swallowed up in the bigger stuff I'm trying to work through. Or, really, sleep through. It also feels private somehow, something between me and him that I feel wrong telling her, and I get a glimmer of what it must be like to be a girlfriend.

There is a pause. It seems like she is weighing the dynamic of the conversation.

"Uh," she says. "I . . . I had sex?" Her voice goes up at the end.

"Are you asking me or telling me?"

"I had sex. With Mike."

Wow. Oh. Okay. In the ten-minute-mile run of sexual activity, she's a varsity cross-country jock and I'm a fat kid at this point.

"Oh," I say. "So now you're, like, A Full Woman."

She rolls her eyes. "Is that how that works?"

I shrug, thinking of my inability to write a sex scene.

"So, uh, how? Did it happen?" I ask.

"I don't know. He invited me over last week, and his mom was out of town at some conference. It just happened."

"Very romantic," I say, and immediately feel bad for snarking.

"It was!" She sounds wounded that I'd shaded her beautiful virginity loss. "He even lit candles and stuff."

"Mike Neckekis lit *sex atmosphere candles*?"

"Yeah."

"Huh. I'm impressed."

"I was too!" she chirps.

"So, then, how was it?"

She stares at the ceiling for a second, takes a breath as she's about to speak, then stops and thinks.

"Good," she says. *"Weird."* Another pause. "Good."

"Did it hurt?"

"It was kind of uncomfortable at first, but no, not really."

"Did it feel, you know, *pleasurable*?"

"Sort of, toward the end."

"You used a condom, right?"

Her head swivels violently toward me. "Do you think I'm an idiot?"

A minute passes. Then she sighs.

"Yeah, no, we totally didn't. I had to go get Plan B."

"Did Mike go with you?"

"He had wrestling practice."

"Did you go by yourself?" I ask, alarmed.

She nods.

"You're kidding. Why didn't you ask me to go with you?"

She looks off to the side and twists her mouth with concern.

"I thought you were mad at me or something."

"What? Why?"

"I don't know. I guess I've felt like that for a while. And then I read that story you wrote."

I feel my face go red, the way it does whenever somebody brings up something I wrote IRL.

"Just because I have a boyfriend now doesn't mean we can't hang out and keep things exactly the way they are," she says softly.

I shake my head, but I don't have the energy to explain why everything's different now, from my feelings about writing to my friendship with Ave. I feel blanched, totally drained of any cleverness or insight. Eventually we both start falling asleep.

While I'm still half-conscious, I dimly register Dawn, backlit from the hallway, quietly pulling my bedroom door closed.

chapter twenty-four

I LOOK DOWN AT the small cluster of fold-out chairs below me, where Ruth's family and a couple of her friends sit. From the front row, Dawn gives me an encouraging nod.

I take a deep breath.

"Okay, so the problem is, it's impossible to write a eulogy because nobody is really honest about who they're writing it for. Theoretically, it's supposed to be for the person who passed away, right? You talk to them in heaven—or, if you're agnostic, you imagine them sitting in the front row with popcorn and Mike and Ikes or something—and tell them how much they enriched your life, how kind and wonderful they were, what a joy to be around. But at their core, eulogies are selfish. They're not for the dead person; they're really for the rest of us, so we can say goodbye the way we would have if we'd seen it coming.

"Which is especially tough in this case because one of so

many things that made Ruth special is that she wouldn't want me to give myself that pass, to turn her into a saintly little old lady whose only interests were fresh Toll House cookies and lumbar back pillows. I think I understand now why people do that: because the pain is less acute if you blur out the idiosyncrasies and specifics of this person you loved and make it more like a generic grief template, like you're saying goodbye to some neutral, safe stranger made out of geriatric Mad Libs.

"The word *eulogy* comes from a combination of the Greek words for praise and elegy. Ruth would call bullshit on both. She'd probably ask for a Viking funeral instead. You know, that kind where you put the body in a canoe and push it into the lake and set it on fire. And she'd want it to scare the crap out of the Melville Prep boys' crew team in the next boat.

"In fact, though, in Judaism, it's sinful to eulogize the dead with attributes they didn't possess. It's considered mocking them. I'm Jewish, so I'm really not allowed to bullshit about her unless I want to be infested with locusts or become a pillar of salt or whatever. So here's the no-BS truth. Ruth was old, and weird, and sometimes super-cranky, and not a lot of people in the neighborhood understood her. Honestly, not a lot of people close to her did, either. I sometimes didn't, for sure. She had a way of knocking people off balance, and if you didn't fall down like most other people, if you rode the wave and kept standing, you were in forever. If you didn't fit in anywhere else, it's almost like she had a you-shaped hole just waiting.

"She was a lot of things to a lot of people who meant more

to her than I did. Before I met her, she was a rebellious daughter and a brave friend. If Ruth's life were a book, I only read the last chapter, except it was upside down and in Esperanto. And she seemed like she was losing it, sometimes. Last year she came over to my house at, like, eight A.M., knocked on my door, and told me, "I'm going to talk to the president." It was her way of trying to tell me that everything would be okay, and I shouldn't worry. She was handling it. But to just tell me that, plainly, like everybody else was telling kids—that everything would be okay—felt like the lie to her. And if she had chosen you as a person in her life, she knew you'd see through it too.

"That was another one of the amazing things about Ruth: She *never* underestimated anybody around her, even when it would be so easy to. And when you're as smart as she was, that's a really incredible, rare way to be.

"It's a little devastating to think about this now—*devastating* is a melodramatic word, I know; I tried a bunch of other ones: *sad*, *depressing*, *disconcerting*, but none of them felt as right— because I wrote off so much of what she said when she was still here without really listening to her, when the whole time she was really telling me everything. She just refused to do it in the typical way. She knew, or at least hoped, everybody she knew was better than that. And we were. But some of us probably didn't know it until now. This isn't fair of me, but I'm mad at her. She was supposed to sit in the waiting room and feel bad for herself and let the rest of us have a proper goodbye. But just because she knew she was about to get called into her appointment, she wasn't about to waste the years she had left. If she didn't, nobody should. And yet, here we are. Right? Using our valuable time just to sit in the waiting room and complain about how bored we are.

"This is the part that she would hate, and I know she'd hate it because during our first-ever conversation, she told me that she didn't want to be thought of as some wise old person, only still alive to teach us all valuable lessons. But maybe the most valuable thing Ruth taught me is the importance of trying to understand people who are different from you, even though it's so much harder than writing them off, because it might make you admit something to yourself that's painful. Sometimes you won't be able to understand, and that's okay. It's the trying, and realizing the importance of trying, that makes a person really special."

I finish reading, my paper blowing a little in the wind at its well-worn crease. To my surprise, almost everybody is in tears, including some of Ruth's family that I've never met and Dawn. Even Avery looks a little tearful.

I flinch when I see my dad in the very last row, sitting straight up like he knows he's in trouble and doesn't want to make it worse. As I climb down from the podium, it's over. Everyone disperses. I stay to help fold and stack the chairs.

Dad jumps in front of me as I carry some chairs to a van, saying, "Scarlett, I know you're furious with me, and I completely understand why."

I say nothing.

"I was just . . . I was a different person. I was really unhappy. So was your mother. And it just happened. I swear I tried to take those lines out, but the editors insisted I leave them in, keep everything as pure and raw as the original manuscript was at the time."

Puuuuuuke.

"I really . . . I'm so sorry, sweetheart. Please, you need to forgive me. I'm devastated."

There are a lot of things I could say to him. Like: Yeah, you were devastated when you got a book deal. You were devastated when it got optioned by a major movie studio. And you were *really* devastated in that online magazine profile that included glossy photos of your apartment and your new wife and daughter, in which I was not mentioned once. But if I've learned anything this week, it's that life is short.

"You're not a good writer," I say and then walk away.

In the car on the ride home, I feel like a raw nerve. Once the floodgate opens, it turns out it's hard to shut it off. It's begun to rain. Dawn keeps looking at me nervously, like she has for the last few days, checking to see that I haven't disappeared or died or something.

"I really hope this doesn't ruin your relationship with your dad," she says tentatively.

"*Wha*—give me six months and maybe a frontal lobotomy, then tell me that."

She nods. We drive in silence, and I flip the radio on. "Fire and Rain," James Taylor, in case I wasn't already in the mood to weep.

"Can I ask you something?"

"Of course."

"I asked Dad once, but it occurred to me that I never asked you. . . . Why did you marry him?"

She says nothing and keeps driving, for a second making me think she didn't hear me.

"He was different than other men I'd dated." She sighs. "Smart. It made me feel special that he picked me."

I feel my heart break more, if possible.

"You didn't need Dad to make you special," I whisper.

She shrugs. "I was working all the time, just so we had money, and I mean *any* money at all, and I guess I couldn't really understand why he couldn't go out and get a job too, just to help me, instead of sitting in there writing every day. But I never said anything, you know? I'd just come home in a really bad mood, and I was angry a lot.

"And the truth is—I'm not just saying this to make you feel bad, because I really don't want you to—when you got older, it was hard because you two were so much alike. You could talk about books, and you had the same crazy imagination and even talk in a similar way, and I just . . . couldn't keep up. I didn't even have the energy to, if I could. I guess it felt sometimes like he was always the good one. And I was always the bad one."

We just drive for a minute, letting it hang there. What can you say that'll make up for years? Nothing adequate.

I just mumble: "It's not like that. I can see now, I was really little, and I was just, I was dumb. I didn't realize."

She nods and says quietly, "I know."

We sit there for a minute, and she says, "He called to explain about the book."

"How could he possibly explain that?"

"I understood. He was mad at me when he wrote that, Scarlett. I was mad at him too, obviously. It wasn't a good situation."

"And you just said it was okay? *Is* it okay?"

"That's not an easy question to answer, really." She keeps her eyes steady on the road. "I mean, yeah, it's fine. I guess there's a lot I have to worry about that's more important than some character based on me ten years ago in a book I won't read. I'm much more upset that he'd do that to you."

I stare out the window.

"You're wrong, though," I say. "I'm more like you than like him."

She shakes her head.

"I am! I work really, really hard. Not at school, but at the stuff I like to do. My eyes are gray like yours. Our voices sound exactly the same on the phone too. Even people we're really good friends with can't tell the difference."

My voice wavers a little bit as I see her start to tear up, but I keep going.

"And I know now how important it is to try your best to understand people. Even people you don't like, or people you don't have anything in common with. And that's all from you. All of that stuff? That means you're smart as hell. Dad's the stupid one."

She swallows hard.

"I'm really sorry, Mom."

A tear rolls down her cheek, and she brusquely wipes it away with the back of her hand, smearing her mascara.

"You don't have to apologize for anything," she says. "I'm so proud of you—exactly who you are, every single day."

When I get home, for the first time since Ruth died, I feel like writing. But not the way I have been. I always rush through stuff. When I read the old installments now, everything seems so flippant, surface-y. Especially the first fic: I cringe when I reread it. How could I have been so catty? And if I stop writing like that, can I even write at all? It'll be hard, but I have to try.

chapter twenty-five

The Ordinaria

The Mullens had no language for it until this year. Its anniversary, if you'd call it that, was coming up—six years—and they'd suddenly begun to discuss it for reasons that Sheila did not like. That night, for instance, over their usual haphazard dinner schedules. She ate at six, then he came home and ate at ten; sometimes she sat with him and had some wine.

Steve sighed heavily, put down his fork down, and said, "It's been . . . you know . . . so long that we've been trying to come to terms with the thing."

They referred to it as "the thing," as in the drive-in movie or some as-of-yet unidentified bumps you'd anxiously notice on your body.

They hadn't said her name in the house for four years. They'd never verbally agreed outright not to, but to say it out loud to each other seemed crude, like an unexpected emotional slur tossed at the other person.

Steve had become a workaholic, spending fifty-five hours a week at the lab developing and then overseeing the global release of the Miss Ordinarias. But, blind with grief he hadn't adequately dealt with, he'd accidentally wound up giving the new products dangerously high levels of empathy, feelings, and life, to somehow make up for the fact that his daughter's had been taken away. Some he focused on more than others.

Sheila mostly just cleaned. She tried to drink enough to develop a problem but wasn't very good at it. After she gave up on that, she'd sometimes go sit by the lake that their daughter used to hang out at, drinking and crushing PBR cans with her friends. In fact, that's what they did that night. In fact, that is why it happened.

She would be twenty-four now, but she made it to only eighteen. For Sheila, the clock stopped right when they saw how slowly the paramedics were walking to the car. She remembered thinking: *They should at least fake running around, moving quickly. We shouldn't have to know before someone tells us who's a professional at telling people.*

This year, though. Almost regularly, with everyone from acquaintances to relatives, The Thing arose. Last weekend it did at Sheila's book club. They were discussing Jodi Picoult, after Sheila was warned that it was a "triggering" book, and a friend of a friend named Gabrielle had too much pinot grigio.

"This is probably inappropriate," slurred Gabrielle. "It's definitely inappropriate, actually, but you've just been so . . . it's been, you know, bad for a really long time." Gabrielle took a deep breath. "I'm not trying to say this way is the best way, but your husband could probably get a good deal on—"

"Do not."

So Sheila wasn't in the mood when Steve said, out of nowhere, even though they both knew exactly what he was talking about, "Sheil, I'm not saying we have one *custom*-made."

"'Made'? Jesus, do you hear yourse—"

"Look. There's a surplus right now of about ten thousand, and a lot of them are in need of a good home."

"In need? Steve, they're like . . . blenders."

"Well . . . they're . . . we went a little too far on this one with the 'human qualities.'" He purposely did not say "I," even though it was utterly his fault and he'd probably get canned any day now.

"So what are you saying? There are ten thousand silicone *orphans* now?"

"Listen to me. Okay? Please, please list—"

"No. Steve? No. Absolutely not. You really think it'd be better if some random . . . robot came in here and slept in her bed and wore her clothes?"

"Nothing else has worked! We're not in a good place!

We haven't been for years, Sheil. It's been . . . just, no talking, no intimacy. Nothing."

Her face fell in horror.

"Oh my *God*, are you using this to try to get a teenage sex robot into our house?"

How could he explain it to her? Why he—vice president of the company, in charge of this new and highly scrutinized product development—irresponsibly tossed out valuable market research results and data and survey feedback on Miss Ordinarias from eighteen-to-twenty-four-year-old men left and right. Why he recklessly deleted notes from the server like "pushiness didn't score well" and "no crude language unless prompted" because all he could hear was his daughter's unique snort-laugh after she told a "your mom" joke, and all he could see were her freckles and the weird way she drank through a straw, sticking it between her index and ring finger and sipping on it. He'd never get his daughter back, so he made her again, in small ways, by the thousands. Sheila would never forgive him.

He dropped his fork with a clatter and put his head in his hands.

Sheila's voice was measured when she asked, "What?"

"Nothing," he said.

* * *

What Steve didn't know was that there was not actually that big of a surplus. Parents had started purchasing the wiped, refurbished Miss Ordinarias—not for their sons but for their friendless daughters. The blinding-white Miss Ordinaria rental places had become as accessible as any Apple Store, and it was unexpectedly lucrative. (There were rentals for one day, one week, one prom date, one school year, one four-year college roommate, one wedding. . . .)

If you were a middle-class seventeen-year-old girl who was weird or different or had health issues, or even were just flat-out unlikable, it was highly likely your parents rented a robot slumber party friend for you that year. If you were upper-middle-class, maybe you kept one through high school. If you were rich, you got yourself a lifetime friendship.

* * *

Scarlett learned this when her father rented her one. His visit was an unexpected surprise. He lived pretty far away, with a whole new family. But as soon as she saw the large white box on the lawn, she knew.

"I just wanted you to see how different you are from—that." He looked encouragingly at Scarlett, and she winced inside thinking about her Ordinaria mom. "Just for a day! And then, if you like it, maybe I can swing a four-year college roommate rental for a graduation gift."

Scarlett looked down, her face burning with humiliation.

"Besides," he asked, "it'll be nice to spend time with someone your own age, won't it?"

"Technically," she said, trying not to let her voice waver, "she is, at the oldest, six."

He left, and Scarlett sat on the lawn with the unwrapped

box and cried, like the biggest spoiled baby ever. Was she that big of a loser? And for that matter, which half of her was the loser—the Ordinaria half or the human half?

She untied the ribbon and opened the white box. The girl inside it immediately sat up, with pale skin and thick straight hair the color of leaves in autumn. Scarlett recognized her from school: She'd belonged to Gideon. She was his eighteenth-birthday present, until his father used Gideon's high profile (this year in *TIME* it was "heir to the Ordinaria Inc. fortune" and "young playboy," a phrase that could not apply to Gideon less) to rent her out for astronomically high rates.

"Hey!" said Ashbot.

Scarlett realized that if Ashbot was a rental now, her memory had been wiped, and she had no idea who Scarlett or Gideon were anymore.

"Um . . . hello."

"So, we're hanging out today, I think, right?"

Scarlett nodded, getting the vague sensation that this interaction wasn't a one-way street: Ashbot was sizing her up too.

"Wanna go to the bookstore?" suggested Ashbot. "Or—oh!—they're playing that French subtitle movie in an art house movie theater in Hamilton; we could go there."

Scarlett wondered if Ashbot was programmed with some background info on Scarlett's likes and dislikes . . . or if Ashbot was just into that stuff. She thought for a moment, bit her lip, and shrugged.

Even Scarlett surprised herself when she asked, "Want to go see that stupid Nicholas Sparks movie?"

"Okay."

After the movie, they sat on a rusty set of kids' swings overlooking the white behemoth of Ordinaria Inc., and together they watched it become dusk. Scarlett felt odd, maybe even a little nauseated. Something was shifting inside her, like someone had put braces on her worldview.

"Do you . . . feel stuff?" asked Scarlett. She was sure the Miss Ordinarias started out uncannily human in the first place . . . but they gained more unique personalities and speech patterns only over time.

Ashbot shrugged and looked away. "Not really."

But it sounded less like a robot's answer and more like the answer of a girl who doesn't want to admit that she does, in fact, have feelings.

"Did you feel stuff today?"

Ashbot thought about it. "Today right before your dad came in, four girls were rented as bridesmaids, *for the same bride*, because she seemed awful and I guess nobody wanted to be in her wedding party, and I felt, maybe angry? And I didn't want to be angry! Only creepy guys rent the angry ones." She shuddered, then looked thoughtful. "I think we sort of feel like . . . always the second-best thing. Like our roles are already decided for us when we're rented, even if it's just for a day."

Scarlett had been so very wrong. She had been wrong

from top to bottom, left to right, her wrongness splattering everywhere like a Pollock painting.

"I'm sorry," Scarlett said.

"For what?" Ashbot asked.

"I, um . . ."

. . . *Militarized an angry mob to chase you off the Pembrooke campus and probably short-circuit you if they had the chance. Underestimated your worth.*

"I just . . . I wasn't very nice to you." Scarlett stared out into the sunset and said softly, "It was just because parts of me are like you. And I didn't like those parts of myself. You know?"

"It's okay." Ashbot nodded. "There are parts of myself I don't like either."

* * *

Scarlett banged on Gideon's door until his father answered. His face immediately curdled.

"My son is busy," he snapped and attempted to shut the door in her face. But it was too late—Gideon was already running down the stairs. He pushed past his father, and he and Scarlett ran to his car. They got in, shut the door, and peeled off.

"What's going on?!" Gideon asked, alarmed, as he turned out of the gated community and onto the main road.

"Do you want Ashbot back?"

"What are you . . . what?"

"Do you want Ashbot back? She's at my house."

"What? No," Gideon snapped, not entirely convincingly. She just looked at him. Finally, he relented: "I don't know."

Scarlett felt the tears spring to the surface but tried to keep breathing.

"Were you upset when your dad took her away?"

Gideon's face indicated that he was more than just upset. He pressed his lips together angrily as he stared out at the road. "My whole life, I swore I'd never be one of those guys who buys an Ordinaria, and now I'm one of them. I'm such a scumbag."

Scarlett shook her head adamantly, and one tear fell— ricocheted, really. A selfish part of her wished she could agree with him that Ashbot was just a machine, that being with Scarlett was way more worthwhile. But it had clearly become a false binary.

"They're not just robots like they used to be. They're different. They're, like . . . real. I don't know how they have feelings, but . . . you didn't do anything wrong. You like a real girl."

"But I like you too." He kept his eyes on the road, refusing to look at her.

She blushed. "Yeah . . . but . . . I mean, we're half 1.0s. Which is just half, but a much older model. Ashbot is a 2.0. Cutting-edge."

They sat there for a minute, both thinking the same thing, until finally she said it in a tiny voice:

"Maybe she's more human than we are."

Gideon didn't respond—he just turned off the main road and merged onto the highway, heading to Scarlett's house.

When they arrived at Scarlett's, though, Ashbot was nowhere to be found.

"At the very least, the rental place is gonna charge my dad a small fortune," Scarlett said, glancing frantically under the sofa's dust ruffle.

"I'm not going to let her be rented out," said Gideon. "I'm just not going to. I don't know if I want to keep her forever, but—"

At that moment, Scarlett's Ordinaria mom came home. She was an older model but a classic bleach-blonde, round-faced and buxom, her fan whirring loudly from overwork—a sound that used to bug Scarlett, but now she didn't mind it. She passed Scarlett and Gideon and sprawled on the sofa. Her battery, as usual, was at 10 percent.

"Are you two talking about that beautiful Miss Ordinaria? Red hair?"

"Yes," they said in unison.

"Oh, yeah, she was with me for a bit, and then she left. I guess your dad thought you needed a friend." Scarlett's mom rolled her eyes, then nudged Scarlett and side-eyed Gideon. "But clearly as long as you're running around with this hunk of man . . ."

"Mom, do not."

She turned to Gideon fondly. "I remember you when you were just a little toddler playing in the backyard kiddie pool naked, waving your—"

"Okay, thanks, Mom. Do you know where she went?" asked Scarlett.

She shook her head.

* * *

Sheila answered the door to find an exquisitely beautiful redheaded teenage girl on her stoop, playing with her hair.

"I'm really sorry," said the girl, "but I was hoping I could use your phone? Mine is dead, and I need to call my rental place."

"Um . . . where'd you park, sweetie? Do you need to get triple A?"

"No, I mean, *I'm* the rental."

And then she laughed *exactly* like her. Exactly.

Sheila felt her face tingle and got dizzy and placed her palms flat on her thighs while bending over slightly, something she'd been taught to do in the frequent moments she felt she might faint. The girl went on.

"'Cause, I think I want to quit, but I don't know if they'll let me. I don't like being a rental anymore."

Stunned, Sheila let her in.

"Do you want me to get you some water?" the girl asked. "I'm really sorry if I did something."

"You didn't."

The girl anxiously filled a glass from the tap and handed it to Sheila.

"Why would you come here just to use a phone?"

"Oh." The girl points to her head. "We have a chip in here with an address, for emergencies. Steve Mullen, VP of

Ordinaria Inc., 428 Donovan Lane—"

"Would you like anything to drink?" Sheila asked faintly. "Please help yourself."

The girl smiled and nodded, then got herself a Diet Coke from the fridge. "Thank you."

"So—you're a Miss Ordinaria rental?" asked Sheila.

The girl nodded.

"What's your name?"

She opened her mouth, then cringed. "I don't like it."

"Can't you just ask for a new one?"

The girl shook her head. "I'm lucky I even have one, even if it's dumb. Most of us just have a product ID. Hey, d'you have a straw?"

Sheila handed her one from the junk drawer and watched as the girl sipped from the straw just like her daughter had— an odd quirk everybody used to make fun of her for. This girl looked nothing like her daughter, but she just *was* her, somehow, in a way Sheila couldn't quite grasp.

Sheila took a deep breath. She couldn't help herself.

"How do you feel about Megan?"

* * *

Once Scarlett and Gideon managed to break into his dad's records, Ashbot was easy to track down. She had been purchased by Steve Mullen, the VP of Ordinaria Inc., and his wife, Sheila.

"Whoa." Scarlett made a *yikes* face. "Is that like, 'rich dude and his wife get a teen sex slave'?"

Gideon suddenly remembered that Steve's daughter's funeral had been around this time of year.

"Oh, shit."

* * *

"So what'd you do today?" Sheila asked through a mouthful of bruschetta. The pasta was still boiling, but they'd already all sat down to eat. Steve was on his computer, as usual.

"Put that away!" Sheila nudged him. His glasses slid down his nose as he reluctantly complied, crunching into his bread in silence. Sheila smiled.

Megan shrugged. "Uhh, I went to class. Soccer practice. We got pizza after."

"What!?" Sheila spread her arms wide. "But I made all this."

"And I'll eat all this. And so will Dad."

Steve's head shot up with a split-second expression of extreme distress, but it immediately disappeared. He nodded assent.

"Yup," he said. "And we can eat the leftovers all week, babe, so don't sweat it."

Sheila put her hand on his arm and rested her head on his shoulder.

"Ewww, stop," said Megan.

The doorbell rang, and Megan jumped up and ran toward the living room, her long hair—now dyed brown—streaming behind her. "Comiiiiiing!"

Megan opened the door and found Scarlett and Gideon standing on the stoop, looking incredibly concerned.

"Hey, can we help you with something?" she asked quizzically.

"We've been looking all over for you, Ashbot!" said Scarlett. Megan winced.

"That's not my name anymore. It's Megan." She shifted uncomfortably. "And my family and I are kind of in the middle of having dinner, so . . ."

"You don't want to do this," Gideon pleaded. "They don't really want you—you're just a replacement. You're gonna have to live in somebody else's shadow."

Megan shook her head, determined.

"I don't care what the reason is. They're nice to me. They act like I'm their *actual* daughter. They're good people, and they were good parents, and what happened to them was unfair. It's not like when I was a rental, when everybody who hired me was some loser who had no friends because they were making the choice to be a shitty person, even though they wouldn't admit it."

Gideon looked at her for a long time, stunned at the level of critical thinking she was able to do. He couldn't deny it; she did seem happier.

"Are you sure?" he whispered.

Megan nodded. Gideon paused, not knowing what to do next. So he just hugged her. "Okay," he mumbled into her hair.

She nodded a farewell to Scarlett and went back inside the warm, bright house where her parents were waiting. She shut the door.

Scarlett and Gideon began to walk back to his car.

"What do we do now?" he asked.

They smiled at each other.

"I guess . . . whatever we want."

chapter twenty-six

IMAGINARY DETECTIVES IS NO *Lycanthrope High*, but it's pretty damn good: Two rogue P.I.s team up to solve crimes that the real cops don't care enough about. Davis is a tall, handsome family man who always follows the rules, and Nickerson is an insanely hot brooding guy who drinks too much, and they're "partners," like in the detective way but also the "as overtly in love as possible on homophobic network television" way. They're so different, but they silently understand each other. My Tumblr is full of gifs of them right now.

When I'm not gushing with Loup about them, I'm hanging out IRL with the Girl Geniuses. I used to think they were just mouth breathers, but Leslie is actually kind of awesome and shockingly vulgar once you get to know her better, and Mike is surprisingly sweet and has random hidden hobbies like building crazy things out of Legos and designing kites. I get why Avery likes him—he's a really nice guy.

But mostly I sit in Ruth's garden. Sometimes I work on it, even though real estate agents will probably be by to show the house any day now. It's looking good. Gardening is a profession, right? Maybe I'll get into that. I like the harmlessness of it, spending your days growing flowers.

As I yank some weeds out of the ground, I suddenly hear a *baa*. Not a distant *baa*. One that almost literally is in my ear.

"Hey."

Gideon is standing at the perimeter of the garden, holding a leash. He looks tentative, which is a strange expression to see on a guy who just walked a sheep down the side of a highway. The sheep's expression is vacant, and I think it's drooling.

"Is that . . . what the fuck, is that a sheep?"

Even as I say it, I know full well that I am staring at a sheep. On a leash.

"Yeah, get it?" he asks, looking absurdly pleased with himself. "You called me a sheep."

"Where did you even get it?"

"Around."

"Oh! Around." That clears everything up.

"Anyway, so, this is an apology. For being . . . you know."

I take a deep breath. "Yeah, look, I—"

The sheep stares dumbly at me. I start laughing.

"I don't mean to look a gift sheep in the mouth, but, um . . .

why did you think this was a good plan? Four legs good, two legs bad?"

He looks surprised. "You don't remember? William. The prom episode."

"Oh. Yeah, of course."

Now you have all of me. It was much more romantic on TV.

BAA, the sheep screams. We both wince, and I shake my head.

"I feel like I can't have a serious conversation right now," I say. "I'm just going to pretend like it's not there. Okay. Ready, set . . ." I turn around and face the door, then summon up all my courage. "Gideon?"

"Yeah?"

"You were right about what you said in the library about me. About testing people. That's why I was so mad. But I was kind of right about you too . . . even though I didn't mean to yell. I was just sad about Ruth."

"You totally were. We were both partly right, I think. I was a colossal dick to you. And to Ashley. I apologized to her too."

Part of me wants to ask if she's okay, but that feels condescending. And besides, Gideon can't speak for Ashley. Instead I decide to stop by the Parkers' tomorrow and say sorry, sans Converse and sans attitude, to see if she wants to hang with me and Ave sometime.

Gideon clears his throat. "I was just wondering how long we're gonna be partly right and entirely mad at each other, because there's an open mic at the Uk Machine tonight, and I'm not gonna go unless you come with me."

I beam stupidly at the door. But I need to give him my bottom line.

"Gideon, the thing is, I . . . really like you." My voice cracks a little. "I really, really like you."

I squeeze my eyes shut.

"I really, really"—he laughs the small laugh of an embarrassed boy discussing strong feelings—"*really* like you."

The audible certainty, as clear as a bell, as final as the post-quiz "Pencils down," gives me chills. I turn back around, sheep be damned.

"Can I also apologize? Or do I need to present a farm animal to you?"

"Go ahead."

"I'm sorry I wrote that stuff," I say.

"I know. It's okay."

BAA, the sheep says and then poops on Gideon's shoes.

"Goddamn it!" he yelps, sidestepping. I double over laughing.

"Fuck!" He shakes most of it off his foot.

"Can you take it . . . back to where it came from?" I wheeze, still cracking up.

"I have it for another half an hour."

"When does the open mic start?"

"Seven."

"So . . . what do we do?"

And I don't mean it like I've meant it, an encoded way of asking: "Are we both weird?" or "Are we both popular?" or "Are we together?" I just mean literally: What are we doing today? Workshopping his new material? Seeing what beachgoers would think of bringing a sheep onto the Jersey Shore? Sneaking into a bad movie so we can make out in the back?

His eyes meet mine.

"I guess whatever we want," he says.

We smile at each other.

BAAAAAAAA.

ACKNOWLEDGMENTS

Grateful to Tina Wexler at ICM, best agent ever, and my editors Jessica Almon and Marissa Grossman for their constant support and excellent instincts. Thanks also to Casey McIntyre, Ben Schrank (whose kind handwritten note still occupies valuable real estate on my fridge), and everyone else at Razorbill/Penguin, plus the trio responsible for the adorable cover: Lindsey Andrews, Michelle Russ, and Chrissy Lau. And to everybody at *Cosmo*, especially Michelle Ruiz, Marina Khidekel, and Joanna Coles.

Thanks to Julie Buntin, Julia Pierpont, Samy Burch, Anna Schumacher, Emily Henry, Elizabeth Minkel and her excellent column on fandom, Hightstown High School for being such an epic piece of shit, Jillian Michaels DVDs, *Buffy,* my dermatologist, Taylor Swift, that shoe over there, laptops, water, doorknobs, and East Village Wines between 9th and St. Marks.

Huge thanks to Greg, my super-supportive and disconcertingly attractive boyfriend, and to my scary-smart little sisters and first readers, Beth and Rebecca. And obviously none of this would have been possible otherwise, so a hundred million thank-yous, Mom and Dad! I'd use your first names, but I don't know them.